LP M CAMILLERI
Camilleri, Andrea, author.
A beam of light

A BEAM
of LIGHT

Center Point
Large Print

Also by Andrea Camilleri and available from Center Point Large Print:

The Brewer of Preston
Game of Mirrors

**This Large Print Book carries the
Seal of Approval of N.A.V.H.**

A BEAM
of LIGHT

Andrea Camilleri
Translated by Stephen Sartarelli

Fountaindale Public Library
Bolingbrook, IL
(630) 759-2102

CENTER POINT LARGE PRINT
THORNDIKE, MAINE

This Center Point Large Print edition is published
in the year 2016 by arrangement with Penguin Books,
an imprint of Penguin Publishing Group,
a division of Penguin Random House LLC.

Copyright © 2012 by Sellerio Editore.
Translation copyright © 2015 by Stephen Sartarelli.
All rights reserved.

Originally published in Italian as *Una lama di luce*
by Sellerio Editore, Palermo.

This is a work of fiction. Names, characters, places,
and incidents either are the product of the author's
imagination or are used fictitiously, and any resemblance
to actual persons, living or dead, businesses, companies,
events, or locales is entirely coincidental.

The text of this Large Print edition is unabridged. In other
aspects, this book may vary from the original edition.
Printed in the United States of America on permanent paper.
Set in 16-point Times New Roman type.

ISBN: 978-1-62899-837-5

Library of Congress Cataloging-in-Publication Data

Names: Camilleri, Andrea. | Sartarelli, Stephen, 1954– translator.
Title: A beam of light : an Inspector Montalbano mystery / Andrea
Camilleri ; translated by Stephen Sartarelli.
Other titles: Lama di luce English
Description: Center Point Large Print edition. | Thorndike, Maine :
Center Point Large Print, 2016. | ©2015
Identifiers: LCCN 2015037822 | ISBN 9781628998375
    (hardcover : alk. paper)
Subjects: LCSH: Montalbano, Salvo (Fictitious character)—Fiction. |
Large type books. | GSAFD: Mystery fiction. | Suspense fiction.
Classification: LCC PQ4863.A3894 L3613 2016 | DDC 853/.914—dc23
LC record available at http://lccn.loc.gov/2015037822

1

Since the first light of dawn, the morning had shown itself to be erratic and whimsical. And so, by contagion, Montalbano's behavior would also prove at the very least unstable that morning. When this happened, it was best to see as few people as possible.

The more the years passed, the more sensitive he became to variations in the weather, just as greater or lesser humidity will affect the pain in an old man's bones. And he was less and less able to control himself, to hide his excesses of cheer and gloom.

In the time he'd taken to go from his house in Marinella to the Casuzza district—about ten miles consisting of dirt paths only good for tanks and of little country roads slightly less wide than a car—the sky had turned from light pink to gray, and then from gray to a faded blue before stopping momentarily at a hazy off-white that blurred the outlines of things and muddled one's vision.

He'd received a phone call at eight o'clock that morning, just as he was finishing his shower. He'd slept late because he knew he didn't have to go to the office that day.

His mood darkened. He hadn't been expecting

any phone calls. Who could it be busting his chops first thing in the morning?

Theoretically, there shouldn't have been anyone at the station other than the telephone operator, since it was supposed to be a special day in Vigàta.

Special in the sense that the illustrious Minister of the Interior, returning from a visit to the island of Lampedusa—where the reception centers for immigrants (yes, they had the gall to call them that!) were no longer in a position to house so much as another one-month-old baby, being packed tighter than a can of sardines—had expressed his intention to inspect the makeshift tent-camps that had been set up in Vigàta, even though these were likewise stuffed to the gills, with the added aggravation that the poor wretches were forced to sleep on the ground and relieve themselves outside.

For this reason Hizzoner the C'mishner Bonetti-Alderighi had mobilized the entire police forces of Montelusa as well as Vigàta to line the streets the high dignitary was to travel, so that his tender ears would not hear the boos, Bronx cheers, and cusswords (called "protests" in proper Italian) of the population, but only the applause of four or five assholes paid for that express purpose.

Without a second thought, Montalbano had dumped the whole business onto the shoulders of Mimì Augello, his second-in-command, and had taken advantage of the situation to enjoy a day off. The mere sight of the Minister of the Interior on television was enough to set the inspector's blood boiling, so he could only imagine what it would be like seeing him personally in person.

The whole thing in the unstated hope that, out of respect for a representative of the government, nobody in Vigàta or environs would kill anybody or commit any other crimes. The criminals would certainly be sensitive enough not to make trouble on a day of such joy.

So who could it be trying to reach him on the phone?

He decided not to answer. But the telephone, after falling briefly silent, started ringing again.

And what if it was Livia? Maybe needing to tell him something important? There was no getting around it: He had to pick up the receiver.

"Hallo, Chief? *Catarella sum.*"

Montalbano froze. Catarella, speaking Latin? What was happening to the universe? Was the end of the world at hand? Surely he must not have heard right.

"Wha'd you say?"

"I sai', 'Catarella 'ere,' Chief."

He breathed a sigh of relief. He'd heard wrong. The universe fell back into place.

"What is it, Cat?"

"Chief, I gatta tell yiz afore anyting ilse 'at iss a long an' compiclated story."

7

Montalbano's foot stretched out and pulled a chair close to him, and he sat down in it.

"I'm all ears, Cat."

"Aright. So, seein' 'at 'iss mornin' yoys truly betooked 'isself onna orders o' 'Specter Augello insomuch as they's aspectin' the 'rrival o' the heliocopter carryin' Hizzoner the Minister o'—"

"Did it arrive?"

"I dunno, Chief. I'm not appraised o' the situation."

"Why not?"

"I'm not appraised cuz I'm not at the scene."

"So where are you?"

"At anutter scene called Casuzza districk, Chief, which is allocated near the ol' railroad crossin' 'at comes after—"

"I know where Casuzza is, Cat. But are you going to tell me what you're doing there or aren't you?"

"Beckin' yer partin', Chief, bu' if ya keep buttin' inna wha' I's sayin' . . ."

"Sorry, go on."

"So anyways, at a soitan point in time the foresaid Isspecter Augello gotta phone call true our swishboard insowhere I's replaced by a replacement, Afficer Filippazzo, foist name Michele, insomuch azza foresaid twissèd 'is leg—"

"Wait a second, who's the aforesaid? Inspector Augello or Filippazzo?"

He shuddered at the thought of Mimì hurting

himself, which would mean he would have to go and welcome the minister himself.

"Filippazzo, Chief, 'oo fer the foresaid reason couldna be prescient fer activist soivice, an' so 'e passed it onna Fazio, 'oo, when 'e 'oid da foresaid phone call, tol' me to fughettabout the aspectation o' the heliocopter ann'at I's asposta go immidiotly at once to Casuzza districk. Which . . ."

Montalbano realized it was going to take half the morning for him to grasp any of what Catarella was saying.

"Listen, Cat, tell you what. I'm gonna fill myself in on this stuff and then call you back in five minutes, okay?"

"But should I keep my sill-phone on or off?"

"Turn it off."

He called Fazio. Who answered right away.

"Has the minister arrived?"

"Not yet."

"Catarella rang me but after talking for fifteen minutes I still hadn't managed to understand a thing."

"I can explain what it's about, Chief. Some peasant called our switchboard to let us know he found a coffin in his field."

"Full or empty?"

"I couldn't quite figure that out. It was a bad connection."

"Why'd you send Catarella?"

"It didn't seem like such a big deal."

He thanked Fazio and called Catarella back.

"Is the coffin full or empty?"

"Chief, the caffin in quession's got iss lid coverin' it an' theretofore the contense o' the foresaid caffin in't possible to know whass inside."

"So you didn't open it yourself."

"Nossir, Chief, issomuch as there warn't no orders consoinin' the raisin' o' the foresaid lid. But if you order me to open it, I'll open it. Bu' iss useless, if y'ask me."

"Why?"

"Cuz the caffin in't empty."

"How do you know?"

"I know cuz the peasant farmer jinnelman 'oo'd be the owner o' the land whereats the foresaid caffin happens a be allocated, an 'ooz name is Annibale Lococo, son o' Giuseppe, an' 'oo's right 'ere aside me, he lifted the lid jess anuff t' see 'at the caffin was accappied."

"By whom?"

"By a dead poisson's body, Chief."

So it was a big deal after all, contrary to what Fazio had thought.

"All right, wait for me there."

And so, cursing the saints, he'd had to get in the car and drive off.

The coffin was the kind for third-class corpses, the poorest of the poor, of rough-hewn wood without so much as a coat of varnish.

A corner of white linen stuck out from under the lid, which had been laid down crooked.

Montalbano bent down to get a better look. Gripping it with the thumb and forefinger of his right hand, he pulled it out a little more and was able to see the initials *BA* embroidered on it and intertwined.

Annibale Lococo was sitting on the edge of the coffin, down near the feet, a rifle on his shoulder, and smoking half a Tuscan cigar. He was fiftyish and sinewy, with sunbaked skin.

Catarella was about one step away but standing at attention, unable to utter a word, overwhelmed by emotion at conducting an investigation alongside the inspector.

All around them, a desolate landscape, more rock than earth, a few rare trees suffering from millennia of water deprivation, shrubs of sorghum, huge clumps of wild weeds. About half a mile away, a solitary little house, perhaps the one that lent the place its name.

Near the coffin, in the dust that had once been earth, one could clearly see the tracks of a small truck's tires and the shoeprints of two men.

"Is this land yours?" Montalbano asked Lococo.

"Land? What land?" said Lococo, screwing up his face at him.

"This land, where we're standing right now."

"Ah, you call this land, sir?"

"What do you grow on it?"

Before answering, the peasant glared at him again, took off his beret, scratched his head, took his cigar out of his mouth, spit on the ground in disdain, then put his Tuscan half-cigar between his lips.

"Nothing. What the hell do you think'll grow on it? Nothing ever takes here. This land's cursed. But I come an' hunt on it. It's full o' hares."

"Was it you who discovered the coffin?"

"Yessir."

"When?"

"This mornin', roun' six-thirty. An' I called you immediately on my cell phone."

"Did you come through here yesterday evening?"

"No, sir, I ain't been true here for tree days."

"So you don't know when they left the coffin here."

"'A'ss right."

"Did you look inside?"

"Of course. Why, didn't you? I's curious. I noticed that the lid wasn't screwed on an' so I lifted it up a little. There's a dead body inside, covered by a sheet."

"Tell me the truth: Did you raise the sheet to have a look at the face?"

"Yessir."

"Man or woman?"

"Man."

"Did you recognize him?"

"Never seen 'im before in my life."

"Do you have any idea why anyone might want to leave a coffin in your field?"

"If I had any ideas like that, I'd start writing novels."

The man seemed sincere.

"All right. Please stand up. Catarella, raise the lid."

Catarella knelt beside the body-box and raised the lid slightly. Then he turned his head suddenly and twisted his mouth:

"*Iam fetet*," he said to the inspector.

Montalbano leapt backwards in astonishment. So it was true! He hadn't heard wrong! Catarella spoke Latin!

"What did you say?"

"I said it already stinks."

Oh no, you don't! This time he'd heard clearly! There was no mistaking it.

"You're trying to fuck with me!" he exploded, deafening himself first and foremost with his shout.

By way of reply, a faraway dog began barking.

Catarella immediately let the coffin lid drop and stood up, red as a rooster.

"Me? Wit' yiz? 'Ow can y'ever amagine such a ting? Never in a million years would I ever . . ." Unable to finish, he buried his face in his hands and started wailing:

"*O me miserum*! *O me infelicem*!"

Montalbano could no longer see straight and lost

control, jumping on Catarella, grabbing him by the neck and shaking him as if he were a tree whose ripest fruit he wanted to make fall to the ground.

"*Mala tempora currunt!*" Lococo said philosophically, taking a pull on his cigar.

Montalbano froze in terror.

So now Lococo was talking Latin too? Had they all gone back in time without noticing? But then how was it that they were wearing modern clothes instead of tunics or togas?

At this point the coffin lid moved from the inside, crashed to the ground with a loud thud, and the corpse, which looked like a mummy, began to stand up very slowly.

"You, Montalbano: Have you no respect for the dead?" the corpse asked, dark with anger as it removed the shroud from its face, becoming immediately recognizable.

It was Hizzoner the C'mishner Bonetti-Alderighi.

Montalbano remained in bed for a long time, thinking about the dream he'd just had and feeling terribly spooked.

Not, of course, because the corpse had turned out to be Bonetti-Alderighi or because Catarella and Lococo had started speaking Latin, but because the dream had been treacherous, deceitful—that is, one of those where the sequence of events follows strict patterns of logic and chronology. And every detail, every element appears in a light that increases the sense of reality. And the boundaries between dream and reality end up becoming too subtle, practically invisible. At least in the last part the logic disappeared, otherwise it would have been one of those dreams where after some time has passed you're unable to tell whether what you remember was real or just a dream.

Except that there wasn't a single thing that was real in the dream he'd just had, not even the arrival of the minister. And therefore, the day that lay ahead was not a day off. He had to go to work. Like any other day.

He got up and opened the window.

The sky was still half blue, but the other half was changing color, tending towards gray, owing to a blanket of flat, uniform clouds coming in from the sea.

He'd just come out of the shower when the phone rang. He went to answer, wetting the floor with the water dripping from his body.

It was Fazio.

"Chief, sorry to bother you, but—"

"What is it?"

"The commissioner called. He just got an urgent communication concerning the Minister of the Interior."

"But isn't he in Lampedusa?"

"Yes, but apparently he wants to come and visit

the emergency camp in Vigàta. He's arriving in about two hours by helicopter."

"What a goddamn pain in the ass!"

"Wait. The commissioner has put our entire department under the command of Deputy Commissioner Signorino, who'll be here in about forty-five minutes. I just wanted to let you know."

Montalbano heaved a sigh of relief.

"Thanks."

"You, I assume, have no intention of attending."

"You're right about that."

"What should I tell Signorino?"

"That I'm sick in bed with the flu and apologize for my absence. And that I'm quite dutifully twiddling my thumbs. When the minister leaves, call me here, in Marinella."

So the minister's visit was real after all.

Did this mean he'd had a prophetic dream? And if so, was he soon going to find the commissioner in a coffin?

No, it was a simple coincidence. There wouldn't be any others. Especially because, if one really thought about it, there was no chance on earth that Catarella would ever start speaking Latin.

The phone rang again.

"Hello?"

"Sorry, wrong number," said a woman's voice, hanging up.

But wasn't that Livia? Why'd she say she had a wrong number? He called her up.

"What's wrong with you?"

"Why do you ask?"

"Sorry, Livia, but you ring me at home, I answer the phone, and you hang up, saying it's a wrong number?"

"Ah, so it *was* you!"

"Of course it was me!"

"But I was so sure you wouldn't be at home that . . . by the way, what are you doing still at home? Are you unwell?"

"I'm perfectly fine! And don't try to dodge the issue!"

"What issue?"

"The fact that you didn't recognize my voice! Does that seem normal to you, that after all these years—"

"They weigh heavy on you, don't they?"

"What weighs heavy on me?"

"All the years we've been together."

In short, they had a nice little row that lasted a good fifteen minutes and more.

Afterwards, he dawdled about the house for another half hour in his underpants. Then Adelina arrived and, upon seeing him, got scared.

"Oh my God, Isspector, wha' ss wrong? You sick?"

"Adelì, don't you start in now too. No, I'm not sick, don't worry. I feel fine. In fact, you know what? Today I'll be eating at home. What are you going to make for me?"

17

Adelina smiled.

"How about I mekka you a nice *pasta 'ncasciata*?"

"Sounds fabulous, Adelì."

"An' enn tree or four crispy fry mullets?"

"Let's say five and leave it at that."

Heaven had suddenly fallen to earth.

He stayed inside for another hour or so, but as soon as an angelic scent began to reach his nostrils from the kitchen, he realized it was hopeless: he would never be able to resist. An empty feeling began to form in the pit of his stomach, the only solution for which was to take a long walk along the beach.

When he returned about two hours later, Adelina informed him that Fazio had called to say that the minister had changed his mind and gone straight back to Rome instead of coming to Vigàta first.

Montalbano got to the station after four o'clock with a smile on his lips, feeling at peace with himself and the entire world. The miracle of *pasta 'ncasciata*.

He stopped for a moment in front of Catarella who, seeing his boss enter, had sprung to attention.

"Tell me something, Cat."

"Yessir, Chief."

"Do you know Latin?"

"O' course, Chief."

Montalbano balked, stunned. He was convinced that Catarella had only made his way, barely, through the compulsory years of schooling.

"Did you study it?"

"Well, I can't rilly say as how I rilly studied it, as far as studyin' goes, but I c'n say I know it pritty good."

Montalbano felt more and more astonished.

"So how did you do it?"

"Do wha', Chief?"

"Come to know Latin?"

"Iss one o' my favorite stories."

"What's one of your favorite stories?"

"The one 'bout Latin an' 'is magic lamp. You know, where the genius comes out an' grannit 'is wishes."

The smile returned to Montalbano's lips. So much the better. Everything was back to normal.

2

On his desk loomed the inevitable mountain of papers to be signed. Among the personal mail that had come in was a letter inviting Inspector Salvo Montalbano to the inauguration of an art gallery that called itself "Il piccolo porto." Launching the new enterprise was a show of twentieth-century painters, the very artists he liked. The letter had arrived late, since the inauguration had already taken place the day before.

It was the first art gallery ever to open in Vigàta. The inspector slipped the invitation into his jacket pocket. He intended to go and check the place out.

A short while later, Fazio came in.

"Any news?"

"Nothing. But there might have been big news."

"What do you mean?"

"Chief, if the minister hadn't changed his mind and had come here, the whole thing would have been a disaster."

"Why?"

"Because the immigrants had organized a violent protest."

"When did you find this out?"

"Just before Commissioner Signorino arrived."

"Did you inform him?"

"Nah."

"Why not?"

"What else could I do, Chief? As soon as he arrived, Signorino had us all line up and advised us all to keep a stiff upper lip and not to create any useless alarms. He told us the television cameras and journalists would be there, and that for this reason we had to be careful to give the impression that everything was working to perfection. So I began to worry that if I were to tell him what I'd been told, he would accuse me of creating useless alarms. So I told our men just to remain on the alert, ready to intervene, but nothing more."

"Well done."

Mimì Augello came in, looking upset.

"Salvo, I just got a call from Montelusa."

"So?"

"Bonetti-Alderighi was rushed to the hospital a couple of hours ago."

"Really? Why?"

"He was feeling bad. Something to do with his heart, apparently."

"But is it serious?"

"They don't know."

"Well, find out and let me know."

Augello left. Fazio's eyes were fixed on Montalbano.

"What's wrong, Chief?"

"What do you mean?"

"The moment Inspector Augello told you the

news, you turned pale. I wouldn't think you'd take it so hard."

Could he possibly tell him that for a second he'd seen Bonetti-Alderighi inside the coffin with the shroud covering his face, just as in the dream?

He answered Fazio rudely, quite on purpose.

"Of course I take it hard! We're men, aren't we? What are we, animals?"

"Sorry," said Fazio.

They stood there in silence. A few moments later Augello returned.

"Good news. Nothing with the heart, nothing serious. Just a case of indigestion. They'll release him this evening."

Montalbano felt quite relieved inside. In the end, there had been no premonitions in his dream.

There wasn't a single visitor in the art gallery, which was located exactly halfway down the Corso. Montalbano felt selfishly delighted; this way he could enjoy the pictures in total comfort. Fifteen painters were on exhibit, each with one painting. From Mafai, Guttuso, and Pirandello to Donghi, Morandi, and Birolli. A real treat.

Out of a small door, behind which there must have been an office, emerged an elegant woman of about forty in a sheath dress—tall, good-looking, with long legs, big eyes, high cheekbones, and long ink-black hair. At first glance, she looked Brazilian.

She smiled at him, then approached, hand extended.

"You're Inspector Montalbano, aren't you? I've seen you on television. I'm Mariangela De Rosa—Marian the gallerist, to friends."

Montalbano liked her immediately. It didn't happen often, but it did happen.

"Congratulations. These are very fine paintings."

Marian laughed.

"A little too fine and expensive for the Vigatese."

"Indeed, I can't imagine how a gallery like yours, here in Vigàta, could—"

"Inspector, I wasn't born yesterday. This show is just to attract attention. The next one will feature engravings—still of high quality, of course—but much more affordable."

"I can only wish you the best of luck."

"Thanks. Can I ask whether there's one painting here that you especially like?"

"Yes, but if you want to persuade me to buy it, you're wasting your time. I'm in no position to—"

Marian laughed.

"Well, it's true, that was a self-interested question, but my only interest was in getting to know you better. I have this belief that I can understand a lot about a man by knowing what painters he likes and what authors he reads."

"I once knew a mafioso, author of some forty

murders, who would weep with emotion in front of a painting by Van Gogh."

"Don't be mean to me, Inspector. Care to answer my question?"

"All right. I like the Donghi painting, but also the Pirandello. Equally. I don't think I could choose between them."

Marian looked at him, then closed the two headlights she had for eyes.

"So you're a connoisseur."

It wasn't a question but a declaration.

"Connoisseur, no. But I know what I like."

"Well, you like the right things. Tell me the truth: Do you have some art at home?"

"Yes, but nothing of any importance."

"Are you married?"

"No, I live alone."

"So will you invite me one day to see your treasures?"

"Gladly. And what about you?"

"In what sense?"

"Are you married?"

Marian pursed her beautiful red lips.

"I was until five years ago."

"How did you end up in Vigàta?"

"But I'm from Vigàta! My parents moved to Milan when I was two and my brother Enrico four. Enrico came back here a few years after graduating, and he now owns a salt mine near Sicudiana."

"And why did you come back?"

"Because Enrico and his wife kept insisting . . . I went through a bad patch after my husband . . ."

"You don't have any children?"

"No."

"What made you decide to open an art gallery in Vigàta?"

"I wanted something to do. But I have a lot of experience, you know. When I was married I had two galleries, small ones, one in Milan and the other in Brescia."

A fiftyish couple came in gingerly, looking around almost as if they feared some sort of ambush.

"How much does it cost?" the man asked from the doorway.

"It doesn't cost anything to enter," said Marian.

The man whispered something into the woman's ear. Then she did the same to him. Whereupon the man said:

"Good evening."

And the couple turned around and went out. Montalbano and Marian started laughing heartily.

When, half an hour later, Montalbano also left the gallery, he'd already made plans to pick up Marian at eight o'clock the following evening and take her out to dinner.

It was a lovely evening, and so he set the table on the veranda and ate the *pasta 'ncasciata* left over from lunch. Then he fired up a cigarette and started contemplating the sea.

After their row that morning, there was little chance Livia would be calling. She would let a good twenty-four hours pass just to let him feel her resentment.

He didn't feel like reading or watching TV. He just wanted to sit there and not think about anything.

But this was surely a hopeless proposition, since his brain refused to remain thoughtless and, on the contrary, kept a good hundred thousand simultaneously in play, unleashing one after the other like rapid-fire camera flashes.

The dream of the coffin. Bonetti-Alderighi's initials embroidered on the shroud. The Donghi painting. Catarella speaking Latin. Livia not recognizing his voice. The Pirandello painting. Marian.

Ah, Marian.

Why had he immediately said yes when she suggested they go out to dinner together? Twenty years earlier he would have answered differently; he would have refused and would have even been surly about it.

Was it perhaps because it was hard to say no to a woman as beautiful and elegant as this one? But hadn't he said no endless times to women even more beautiful than Marian?

This could only mean one thing. That his personality had undergone a change due to aging.

The reality was that nowadays he very often felt lonely, and he was tired of feeling lonely, bitter about being lonely.

He knew perfectly well that if he dragged certain nights out by smoking and drinking whisky on the veranda, it wasn't because he couldn't sleep, but because it really bothered him that he was sleeping alone.

He wished he had Livia at his side, but if it couldn't be Livia, any other good-looking woman would do.

And the strange thing about this desire was that there was nothing sexual about it. He wished only that he could feel the warmth of another body next to his. He remembered the title of a film that expressed this desire perfectly: *To Sleep Next to Her*.

He didn't even have any friends he could really call friends. The kind you can confide in, the kind to whom you can reveal your innermost thoughts. Fazio and Augello were certainly his friends, but did not belong to this category.

Disconsolate, he stayed out on the veranda to finish the bottle of whisky.

Every so often he nodded off but then would wake up barely fifteen minutes later, feeling more and more melancholy, more and more convinced he'd done everything wrong in life.

If only he'd married Livia when he should have . . .

For heaven's sake, let's not start in with any stocktaking.

Let's call a spade a spade: If he'd married Livia they would have broken up after a few years of marriage. He was as sure of this as he was of his own death.

He knew himself well, and he knew he had neither the will nor the ability to adapt to another person, not even someone he loved as much as Livia.

Nothing—not love, not passion—would have been strong enough to force them both to spend the rest of their lives under the same roof.

Unless . . .

Unless they had adopted François, as Livia had wanted.

François!

François had been a total failure. The kid had done his best to make sure the situation worsened, but he and Livia had delivered the coup de grâce.

Back in 1996 they'd had to take a little Tunisian orphan of ten into their home for a short while. François was his name, and they'd grown so fond of him that Livia had suggested they adopt him. But Montalbano hadn't felt like it, and so the kid ended up going to live on the farm of Mimì Augello's sister, where he was treated as one of the family.

Viewed with the hindsight of many long years, this may have been a big mistake.

The agreement was that he would send Mimì's sister a check each month to help pay expenses. He'd instructed his bank to take care of this, and it had gone on for years.

The problem was that the older François got, the more difficult he became. Disobedient and belligerent, always surly and complaining, he didn't even want to hear about studying. And yet he was extremely intelligent. In the early going, Livia and Salvo went to see him often; then, as often happens, the visits became fewer and farther between, until they stopped going altogether. But for his part, the kid refused to go to Vigàta to see Livia when she would come down from Genoa.

Clearly François suffered from his situation and maybe had even taken the fact that they hadn't adopted him as a rejection. A few days after the boy's twenty-first birthday, Mimì Augello told Montalbano that François had run away from the farm.

They searched for him over land and sea, but never found him. And so they'd all had to resign themselves.

Now that he was twenty-five, it was anybody's guess where he hung his hat.

But why go over the past again? What was broken couldn't be fixed.

The thought of François brought a lump to his throat. He dissolved it by downing the last quarter of the bottle of whisky.

At the first light of dawn he saw a majestic three-master on the horizon, heading for the harbor.

He decided to go to bed.

When he woke up, Montalbano realized he was in a dark mood. He went to open the window. As if to prove the point, the sky was gloomy, completely covered with dark gray clouds.

Catarella stopped him on his way in.

"'Scuse me, Chief, but there's a jinnelman waitin' f'yiz."

"What's he want?"

"'E wants to report a armed assault."

"But isn't Augello around?"

"'E called sayin' 'e's gonna be late."

"What about Fazio?"

"Fazio's betooken hisself to Casuzza."

"Why, was another coffin found?"

Catarella gave him a bewildered look.

"Nah, Chief, iss cuzza some kinda nasty fight 'tween two hunners an' one o' them, I dunno which, if i' wuzza foist or the seccon', shot th'other, an' so, consequentially, I dunno if i' wuzza foist or the seccon' 'at got wounded inna leg, but jest a li'l, jest a grazin' wound."

"All right. What did this gentleman say his name was?"

"I can't rilly remember, Chief. Sumpin' like di Maria or di Maddalena, sumpin' like 'at."

"The name's di Marta, Salvatore di Marta," said a well-dressed man of about fifty, generously doused in cologne, completely bald, and shaven to perfection.

Martha, Mary, and Magdalen, the Pious Women of Calvary. Catarella got it wrong, as usual, but he was close.

"Please come in and sit down, Signor di Marta."

"I'd like to report a case of armed assault."

"Tell me what happened, and when it happened."

"Well, my wife came home past midnight last night—"

"Excuse me for interrupting, but who was assaulted, you or your wife?"

"My wife."

"And why didn't she come in person to file the report?"

"Well, Inspector, Loredana is very young, not quite twenty-one years old . . . She got very frightened, and even seems to have a little fever . . ."

"I understand. Go on."

"She got home late last night because she'd gone to see her best friend who wasn't feeling well, and she didn't have the heart to leave her all alone . . ."

"Of course."

"In short, as soon as Loredana turned onto Vicolo Crispi, which is very poorly lit, she saw a man lying on the ground and not moving. She stopped the car and got out to give the man assistance, but then he suddenly stood up, holding something that looked to her like a gun, and he forced her back into the car and sat down beside her. Then—"

"Just a minute. How did he force her? By pointing the gun at her?"

"Yes, and he also grabbed her by the arm, so hard that it left a bruise. He must have been very violent, since he also bruised her shoulders when he pushed her into the car."

"Did he say anything?"

"Who, the attacker? No, nothing."

"Was his face covered?"

"Yes, he had a kind of bandana covering his nose and mouth. Loredana had left her purse in the car. He opened it, took out the money that was inside, took the keys out of the ignition and threw them out into the street, far away, and then . . ."

The man was clearly upset.

"And then?"

"And then he kissed her. Actually, more than kiss her, he bit her twice on the lip. You can still see the marks."

"Where do you live, Signor di Marta?"

"In the new residential neighborhood called I Tre Pini."

Montalbano knew the area. There was something about this that didn't make sense.

"I'm sorry, but you said the attack occurred in Vicolo Crispi."

"Yes, and I think I know what you're getting at. You see, when I got home yesterday, I hadn't been able to deposit the supermarket's receipts in the night safe of my bank. And so I gave the money to Loredana and asked her to be sure to deposit it before going to her friend's house. But she forgot to, and only remembered when she was on her way home, and that was why she had to take that detour which—"

"So there was a lot of money in your wife's purse?"

"Yes, a lot. Sixteen thousand euros."

"Was the guy satisfied with only the money?"

"He kissed her too! And it's a good thing he limited himself to one kiss, even if it was violent!"

"That's not what I was referring to. Does your wife usually wear jewelry?"

"Well, yes. A necklace, earrings, two rings . . . A little Cartier watch . . . All valuable stuff. And her wedding ring, naturally."

"The attacker didn't take any of it?"

"No."

"Do you have a photo of your wife?"

"Of course."

He took it out of his wallet and handed it to Montalbano, who looked at it and gave it back.

Fazio came in.

"Just in time," said the inspector. "Signor di

Marta is going to go into your office now and file an official report of an armed assault and robbery. Good-bye, Signor di Marta. We'll be back in touch with you soon."

How does a man some fifty-odd years old manage to marry a girl not yet twenty-one? And not just any young girl, but one like Loredana who, to judge from the photo, was so beautiful it was almost frightening?

How did the guy manage not to realize that by the time he was seventy, his wife would be barely forty? In other words, still desirable and with her own solid, healthy desires?

Okay, it was true he'd spent the previous night crying over his loneliness, but a marriage like that would be a cure worse than the disease.

Fazio returned some fifteen minutes later.

"So what supermarket does the guy run?" the inspector asked.

"The biggest one in Vigàta, Chief. He married one of the checkout girls last year. People around town say he lost his head over her."

"Does this story make any sense to you?"

"No. Does it to you?"

"No."

"Can you imagine a thief taking only the money and not grabbing the jewelry as well?"

"No, I can't. But it's still possible we've got it wrong."

"Do you believe in gentlemen thieves?"

"No, but I do believe in desperate people who suddenly turn to robbery but wouldn't know where to resell stolen jewelry."

"So how do you want me to proceed?"

"I want to know everything about this Loredana di Marta. What her best friend's name is and where she lives, what her habits are, who her friends are . . . Everything."

"Okay. Do you want me to tell you about that little hunters' quarrel in Casuzza?"

"No. I don't want to hear anything about Casuzza."

Fazio looked perplexed.

3

After Fazio left, the inspector resumed his bureaucratic labors, signing page after page. Finally, by the grace of God, it was time to eat.

"You cheated on me yesterday," Enzo reproached him as soon as he came into the trattoria.

"I ate at home. Adelina cooked for me," Montalbano quickly replied, to forestall any fits of jealousy on Enzo's part. Having the inspector as a regular customer was very important to the restaurateur.

For some reason, the story that Signor di Marta had told him had dispelled his bad mood. Deep down, the man had practically been asking for his wife to cheat on him. Not that the inspector was in the habit of taking pleasure in others' misfortunes, but all the same . . .

"What've you got for me?"

"Whatever you want, Inspector."

He ordered and was served. He may even have abused his power: He ordered too much, and repeatedly. So much, in fact, that he even had a little trouble getting up from his chair.

A stroll along the jetty, ever so slowly, one foot up, one foot down, thus became a dire necessity.

The handsome three-master he'd seen heading for the port in the early morning was now moored in the berth where every day at eight p.m. the postal boat docked. Apparently it would have to put back out to sea before that hour.

Two sailors were busy swabbing the deck with buckets and mops. No other crew members or passengers were visible. Astern, on the side of the boat, was the name: *Veruschka*. It was flying a flag that Montalbano didn't recognize. On the other hand, how many Italian moneybags flew the Italian flag on their yachts? He vaguely recalled that there was a famous model named Veruschka many years ago.

He sat down as usual on the flat rock beneath the lighthouse and lit a cigarette.

Halfway down the rock he noticed a crab that was staring at him without moving.

Was it possible that for all these years he had been harassing the same crab by throwing pebbles at it?

Or was it perhaps a family of crabs that had passed the word on from father to son?

"Look, Junior, almost every afternoon Inspector Montalbano comes around here to play with us. Just indulge him and let him get his jollies. He's a lonely old bastard who means no harm."

He stared back at the crab and said:

"Thanks, crab, but I don't feel like it today. Sorry."

The crab moved and started walking sideways to the edge of the rock, then vanished into the water.

Montalbano wished he could stay there until sunset.

But he had to return to the office. He got up, sighing, and started heading back.

As soon as he'd passed the three-master's gangway, three taxis in a row arrived and pulled up beside the boat. Apparently the passengers had wanted to visit the Greek temples.

He spent the whole afternoon boring himself to death signing useless papers. But he absolutely had to do it, not out of any sense of duty but because he'd learned that the subtle vengeance of an unsigned paper was to multiply into at least two other sheets, in one of which he was asked to explain why he hadn't signed the previous one, while the other was a copy of the first, just in case he had never received it.

Around seven in the evening, Fazio returned, looking like a disappointed hunter coming home with nothing in his game bag.

"Chief, I got some info on Loredana di Marta."

"Let's have it."

"It's not much. The girl, whose maiden name is La Rocca, is the daughter of Giuseppe La Rocca and Caterina Sileci; she was born in . . ."

Fazio was off and running with his usual obsession, which was to recite the entire records-office file of a person under investigation. If Montalbano didn't stop him at once, the guy was liable to go back to the girl's great-grandparents. He threatened him with a dirty look.

"Hold it right there. I'm warning you: If you continue to indulge in your records-office mania, I swear I'll—"

"Sorry, Chief. I'll stop. As I was saying, before marrying di Marta, this Loredana had been the girlfriend of a certain Carmelo Savastano, a debauched good-for-nothing. They'd been together since she was fifteen and he was twenty. Apparently she was hopelessly in love with him."

"So why'd she leave him for di Marta?"

Fazio shrugged.

"Who knows? But there's a rumor going around."

"Let's hear it."

"That di Marta made a deal with Savastano."

"Let me get this straight. He told Savastano to leave her?"

"So they say."

"And Savastano accepted?"

"Yes, he did."

"I guess he was well paid."

"Well, he certainly wasn't persuaded by words alone."

"So di Marta basically bought Loredana. What do people in town say about her?"

"Nobody has a bad word to say about her. They all say she's a good girl. Well behaved. She goes out only with her husband or to visit her girlfriend."

"Do you know what that girl's name is?"

"Yes. Valeria Bonifacio. She lives in a free-standing house in Via Palermo, number 28."

"Is she married?"

"Yes. To the captain of a ship who spends months on end at sea before returning to Vigàta."

"So, in conclusion, it really was a case of assault with a deadly weapon?"

"Apparently."

"Which means we have to start looking for the robber."

"Which won't be easy."

"I agree."

As soon as Fazio went out, the inspector had an idea. He called up Adelina, his housekeeper.

"Wha'ss wrong, Isspector? Somethin' happen?"

"No, everything's fine, Adelì, calm down. I need to talk to your son, Pasquale."

"He jessa wenn out. I have 'im a-call you when'e comma beck."

"No, don't bother, Adelì. I'm about to leave my office and I won't be home tonight either. It's better if he calls me tomorrow morning, here at the station."

"Okay, whatteva you say, Isspector."

Pasquale was a habitual offender, a house burglar constantly in and out of prison. Montalbano became the godfather of Pasquale's young son at the baby's baptism, and in a gesture of gratitude, they named the boy Salvo. Every so often the inspector turned to Pasquale for useful information.

Why was the metal shutter of the gallery lowered almost to the ground?

And yet it was five minutes to eight. Had Marian forgotten about him and their date?

Feeling discouraged, he rang the doorbell. A moment later he heard her voice say: "Raise the shutter and come on in."

The first thing he saw as he entered was that there were no more paintings on the walls.

He didn't have time to say anything before Marian came running up to him, embraced him, grazed his lips with hers, stepped back laughing, and then did a pirouette like a dancer.

"What's going on?" Montalbano asked.

"I sold all the paintings! All at once! Come."

She took his hand, led him into the office, sat him down in an armchair, opened a mini-fridge, and pulled out a bottle of champagne.

"I bought it just for the occasion. I was waiting for you, so we could have a toast. Please uncork it."

Montalbano uncorked the bottle while she went and got two glasses.

They toasted. Montalbano was happy that she was happy.

This time Marian held out her lips for him, and

Montalbano placed an ever so chaste kiss on them. Then she sat down in the other armchair.

"I'm happy," she said.

Happiness made her more beautiful.

"Tell me how it happened."

"Around ten-thirty this morning a very elegant lady more or less my age came in. She spent a whole hour looking at the paintings, and then complimented me on her way out."

"Was she Italian?"

"I don't think so. She spoke perfect Italian, but with an accent that sounded German to me. She came back fifteen minutes later with a man who looked about sixty, obese but very distinguished. He introduced himself as Osvaldo Pedicini, an engineer, and said that his wife wanted to buy all the paintings on exhibit. I very nearly fainted."

"Then what happened?"

"He asked me to name a price. I did some math and gave him a figure. I was expecting to have to bargain, but he didn't bat an eyelash. But he said he was in a hurry. So I closed everything up and we went to the bank. He spoke with the manager, and they made some calls. I used some excuse to go out and went and had a cognac at a bar. I could barely stand up from the shock of it all. When I returned, the bank manager and Pedicini said I should come back at three."

"What did you do?"

"Nothing. I was incapable of doing anything.

My mind was confused. It all seemed so incredible. I just waited here, in this armchair. I wasn't hungry. Just very thirsty. Then at three I went back to the bank. Only Pedicini was there; his wife hadn't come. The manager assured me that everything had been taken care of, and that I would have my money tomorrow, but I could consider it already in the bank. So we came back here, and I found three taxis stopped outside the gallery. Two sailors brought in some crates and packaged all the paintings under Pedicini's direction. By six it was all done."

She got up and refilled their glasses, then sat back down and extended one of her legs towards Montalbano.

"Pinch me."

"Why?"

"So I can be sure I'm not dreaming."

Montalbano bent forward, reached out, and executed a sober, gentlemanly squeeze of her calf, but then jerked his hand back as if he'd received a shock. Marian was vibrating. The nerves beneath her skin were like so many little snakes. An uncontrollable energy emanated from her.

"I owe everything to you," she said.

"To me?!"

"Yes. You brought me good luck."

She stood up and came and sat on the arm of Montalbano's easy chair, putting her arm around his shoulders.

Her body gave off warmth and scent. The inspector immediately began to sweat.

Perhaps it was best to go out and get a breath of air, to relieve the tension that with each passing moment became more dangerous.

"Has your appetite returned?"

"Yes. And how."

"Then tell me where you'd like to go, and—"

"First let's finish the bottle."

Apparently Marian had other things in mind.

"Have you told your brother what happened?"

"No."

The answer was immediate and blunt.

"Why not?"

"Because Enrico and my sister-in-law would have rushed right over here."

"So?"

She said nothing.

"You don't want to see them?"

"Not tonight."

You couldn't get any clearer than that! Shouldn't he perhaps nip this in the bud before things got more complicated?

Meanwhile, it was utterly imperative that he not get drunk.

"Listen, Marian, we can't finish the bottle."

"What's preventing us?"

"We have to drive."

"Oh, right," she said, frowning in disappointment. "Too bad. Excuse me for just a moment."

She got up, opened a little door, behind which Montalbano got a quick glimpse of a bathroom, then went inside and locked the door.

The moment lasted half an hour. Then Marian came back out, newly made up and fresh as a rose.

"What do you feel like eating?"

"Whatever you do."

"I think it's better if we go in separate cars. Mine is parked right here in front."

"So is mine. Oh, I wanted to tell you something. There's a nonnegotiable condition to my coming out to dinner with you."

"And what's that?"

"It's on me. I have to celebrate."

"No, come on."

"Then no deal."

She was serious. And firm. Montalbano didn't want this to drag on.

"All right then."

They went out. The inspector helped Marian roll down the shutter. Then she pointed to a green Fiat Panda.

"That's my car."

"Okay, just follow me," said Montalbano, heading for his car.

He wanted to take her to that trattoria at the water's edge where they served great quantities of antipasto, but he made two wrong turns. After a while he gave up, realizing he had no idea where he was or where he should go. He stopped the car. Marian pulled up beside him.

"Can't find the way?"

"No."

"But where are we supposed to be going?"

"There's a restaurant that serves all kind of antipasti that—"

"I know that place! Follow me."

How humiliating.

Ten minutes later they were sitting down at a table.

"Did your brother take you here?" Montalbano asked.

"No. Someone else," she replied, cutting him short. Then she said: "I want to know everything about you. How come you're not married? Are you divorced? Engaged?"

It was a good opportunity. He talked to her at length about Livia, and when he was done she made no comment.

Montalbano was pleased to see that she ate with gusto and left nothing on her plate.

She told him about a marriage gone wrong and the difficulties she had to overcome to get a divorce.

"If you fell in love with another man, would you remarry?"

"Never again," she said decisively.

Then she smiled.

"You're sharp. One can tell you're a cop."

"I don't understand."

"You've started your questioning with a specific goal in mind."

"Really? And what would that be?"

"To find out whether there've been any other men in my life since the divorce. Yes, there have been, but they were all brief affairs of no importance. Happy?"

Montalbano didn't answer.

Then out of the blue she said:

"Tomorrow, I'm sorry to say, I have to go away. But first I'm going to stop in at the bank to make sure everything's in order. We won't be able to see each other for at least a week."

"Where are you going?"

"To Milan."

"To see your parents?"

"I'll certainly see them, yes. But I'm going because Pedicini told me something that interested me very much."

"Care to tell me what?"

"Sure, it's not a secret. He wants me to find him some seventeenth-century paintings of value. He and his wife will be back in Vigàta in a couple of weeks. He gave me the name of a gallerist friend of his in Milan who might be able to help me. Are you sorry?"

"A little."

"Only a little?"

Montalbano preferred to dodge the question.

"I'm afraid I don't understand."

"Don't understand what?"

"If Pedicini is a friend of this gallerist, why does he need you as a go-between?"

"Pedicini told me he doesn't want to get personally involved, not even with his friend." Then, caressing the back of his hand: "I feel like getting drunk."

"You can't. Don't forget you have to drive."

"Ouf! Then I'm going to pay the bill right away and we can go. We're finished, aren't we? There's no room left in my stomach, not even for a single clam."

Montalbano asked the waiter for the bill.

"Do you want to go home?" he asked.

"No."

"Where do you want to go?"

"To your place. Got anything to drink?"

"Whisky."

"Excellent. Anyway, I want to see your paintings."

"I don't own any paintings. Only engravings and drawings."

"That's just as good."

The veranda sent her into ecstasy.

"God, it's so beautiful here!"

She sat down on the stone bench and gestured impatiently for Montalbano to sit down beside her.

"Didn't you want to see my—"

"Later. Come here."

Oh, well. The best he could do was play for time.

"I'll go and get the whisky."

He went and returned with a new bottle and two glasses.

"Would you like some ice?"

"No. Sit down."

He sat down. He reached for the bottle to unscrew the cap but was immediately prevented by Marian, who embraced him and kissed him. Long and hard.

She then released him and laid her head on his shoulder. Montalbano poured half a glass and handed it to her.

She didn't take it.

"I don't feel like getting drunk anymore. I want to remain perfectly lucid."

Montalbano drank the half-glass in her place, downing it in two gulps, in hopes of recovering from the mental and physical disorientation her kiss had caused him.

But he could tell that Marian was troubled. In fact she stood up.

"Let me by."

Montalbano got to his feet, and as soon as she was in front of him, she grabbed his hand and led him away.

They stepped down from the veranda. Marian took off her shoes.

They walked down the beach to the water, hand in hand.

Then she let go of him and started running along the water's edge, laughing.

Montalbano started running after her, but she was faster. He gave up.

Marian disappeared into the darkness.

The inspector turned around and started heading back.

He didn't hear her come up behind him.

He just felt himself grabbed roughly by the waist and turned around, as she pressed her whole body up against him, panting, trembling, and whispered in his ear:

"Please, please. I swear that afterward I won't . . ."

This time it was Montalbano who took her by the hand and started running towards the house.

4

He woke up with a start and looked at the clock in the light filtering through the slats in the shutters. Seven o'clock. He immediately remembered everything that had happened. And he felt deeply disturbed by it. In "day after" scenarios in the past, he had felt shame and remorse upon awakening. But not this time. This time was quite different. Over the course of the night, something unexpected had happened between the two of them. And the feeling frightened him.

He sat up in bed. The place beside him was desolately empty, as nearly every morning. He shut his eyes again, lay back down, and sighed, unable to put in any kind of order the contradictory and confused feelings clogging his brain.

At any rate, the fact was that Marian had got out of bed and gone into the bathroom, got dressed, and left, and he hadn't heard a thing, dead to the world in a tomblike sleep.

He'd been swept away by a cyclone, a veritable equatorial tempest that had gone on for a long time—a storm by which, just to be clear, he had been delighted to be carried away, and which in the end had left him utterly breathless and drained of strength, like a castaway who finally reaches the shore after swimming desperately without end.

He felt a surge of pride. Good God! Considering all the years he was carrying around, when you came right down to it . . .

But it was time for him to get up too.

Quite unexpectedly, the wonderful smell of fresh-brewed coffee reached his nostrils.

Had Adelina come early?

"Adelì!"

No answer. He heard footsteps approaching.

Then Marian appeared, all dressed and ready to go out, with a cup of coffee in her hand.

He remained spellbound as he watched her draw near. And the feeling that so frightened him returned, powerful and unstoppable.

Marian set the cup down on the bedside table, smiled a happy smile, then bent down and kissed him.

"Good morning, Inspector. It's so strange. I can make my way around your house as if I've always known it."

By way of reply, Montalbano's body acted on its own, without involving his brain in the least.

He leapt out of bed and held her body tight in a mixture of renewed desire, tenderness, and gratitude.

She returned his kisses vigorously, but at a certain point stepped away, firm and decisive.

"Please stop."

Montalbano's body obeyed.

"You don't know what I would give to be able to stay," said Marian. "Believe me. But I really have to go. I also slept in, and I'm late. I'll try to return to Vigàta as soon as I can . . ."

She took a cell phone out of her pocket.

"Give me all your numbers. I'll call you tonight from Milan."

Montalbano walked her to the door.

He still hadn't been able to say a word. He was in the grips of an emotion that prevented him from speaking. She threw her arms around his neck, looked him straight in the eye, and said:

"I didn't know I . . ."

Then she quickly turned around, opened the door, and went out.

Montalbano, who was naked, just stood there, head poking out of the door, and watched her get in the car and drive off.

As he was heading back to the bedroom, the house seemed much emptier than before.

He immediately wished Marian was back. Then he threw himself onto the bed on the side where she had slept, burying his face in her pillow to get another whiff of her flesh.

He'd been in the office for five minutes when the phone rang.

"Chief, I got the son o' yer 'ousekipper, meanin' Adelina, natcherilly, onna line."

"Put him on."

"Mornin', Inspector. Pasquale here. Mamma tol' me you wannit a talk to me. Anything wrong?"

"How's my godson Salvo doing?"

"Growin' like a dream."

"I need some information."

"Always glad to help . . ."

"Have you heard anything about a mugger who robbed a lady at gunpoint in Vicolo Crispi? He took her money but not her jewelry, then he kissed her—"

"He kissed 'er?"

"That's right."

"An' 'e din't do nothin' else?"

"No."

"I'm shocked."

"You haven't heard any mention of it?"

"No, I don't know nothin' about it. But if you want, I can ask around."

"You'd be doing me a big favor."

"I'll ask around and get back to you, Inspector."

Mimì Augello and Fazio came in together.

"Any news?" the inspector asked.

"Yes," said Augello. "Last night, not five minutes after you left, a certain Gaspare Intelisano came in to report a crime."

"What was the crime?"

"Well, that's just it. Normally a person comes in to report that someone broke into his house or something, whereas this time it was just the opposite."

"I haven't understood a thing."

"That's the point. It seemed like a delicate matter, and complicated, and so I asked him to come back the following morning, when you'd be here. It's better if he talks with you. Anyway, he's here now, waiting for you to arrive."

"But just tell me a little beforehand!"

"Believe me, you'll understand a lot more if he tells you himself."

"Oh, all right."

Fazio went out and came back with Intelisano.

He was about fifty, tall and slender, with a little white beard that looked like a goat's, and shabbily dressed in trousers, a threadbare green velvet jacket, and clodhopping peasant boots. He was visibly nervous.

"Please sit down and tell me everything."

Intelisano sat down at the outermost edge of the chair, mopping his sweaty brow with a handkerchief as big as a bedsheet. Mimì pulled up in the chair in front of him, and Fazio went and sat at the little table with the computer.

"Shall I put this on the record?"

"Let Signor Intelisano start talking a little first," Montalbano replied, looking at the visitor.

Intelisano sighed, mopped his brow again, and asked:

"Do I have to start by giving my name, date of birth, and—"

"For the moment, no. Just tell me what happened."

"Mr. Inspector, let me start by sayin' that I'm the sole owner of three large pieces of land my father left me, which are planted mostly with wheat and vines. I hang on to them just so as not to dishonor my late father, rest his soul, because it costs more than I earn. One of these properties is in the district of Spiritu Santo, and it's a big pain in the ass."

"Why? It doesn't produce?"

"Half of it's productive, and half is barren. The good half is planted with wheat and fava beans. But the pain in the ass is that the boundary between Vigàta's territory and Montelusa's runs right through it, and so it's registered in two different towns, and every so often there's a big confusion with municipal taxes and duties and so on. Know what I mean?"

"Yes. Go on."

"I hardly ever go to the barren part. What am I gonna do there? There's a little house with the roof caved in and no door, a few bitter almond trees, and nothing else. Yesterday morning as I was on my way to the good part of the property, I suddenly needed to take a leak as I was passing by. So I decided to go into the house, but I couldn't."

"Why not?"

"Because someone had put a door on the house, made of strong wood, and locked it with a padlock."

"Without you knowing anything about it?"

"Right."

"You're telling me someone went there and put up a door where there wasn't one before?"

"That's right."

"So what did you do?"

"I remembered that there's a little window in the back of the house. So I went to look. But I couldn't see inside because they'd covered it up from the inside with a board."

"Do you have any farmhands working for you who—"

"I do. I've got two Tunisians workin' for me on the Spiritu Santo property. They didn't know nothin' about the door. It's a big property and the part that they work on is pretty far from the little house. An' I'm sure that whoever put the door there did it at night."

"So you have no idea whether they turned the house into a residence or storage facility?"

"Well, to be honest, I think I do have an idea."

"Tell me."

"I'm sure they made a storehouse out of it."

"What makes you think that?"

"In front of the house there's some tire tracks, a lot of 'em, that look like they're made by a Jeep or somethin' similar."

"Is the door very big?"

"Just big enough for a big crate to pass through."

A thought flashed through Montalbano's head. A little house. *Casuzza* in Sicilian. Casuzza district. A crate. A coffin. Tire tracks in the dusty ground. Was there any connection with his dream?

This was perhaps why he said:

"I think it's best if we go and have a look."

Then he had second thoughts.

"Is the house on the part of the property in Vigàta's territory or in Montelusa's?" he asked.

"Vigàta's."

"So it's in our jurisdiction."

"Want me to come too?" asked Augello.

"No, thanks, I'll go with Fazio."

Then, turning to Intelisano:

"Think one of our cars can make it out there?"

"Bah! Maybe with a good driver . . ."

"All right, then, we'll go with Gallo. Signor Intelisano, I'm sorry, but you have to come with us."

Miraculously, Gallo managed to take them all the way to the little clearing in front of the house. But it was like being on a roller coaster for a whole hour, with your stomach about to come out of your nostrils.

Montalbano and Fazio looked first at the house and then at Intelisano, who was standing stock-still with his mouth open.

There was no door. Nothing preventing people

from entering. Whoever wanted to go inside could freely do so.

"Did you dream it?" Fazio asked Intelisano.

The man shook his head emphatically.

"There was a door, I tell you!"

"Look down before speaking," Montalbano said to Fazio.

There were a lot of very visible tracks made by large tires, crisscrossing in the dusty ground.

Montalbano went up to the entrance, where there was supposed to have been a door, and looked carefully around.

"Signor Intelisano is telling the truth. There was a door here," he said. "There are recent traces of quick-drying cement between the stones where they'd put the hinges."

He went in, followed by Intelisano and Fazio.

Half the roof was caved in. The entire house consisted of a single, large room, and in the part still protected by the roof there was a great quantity of straw piled up.

Upon seeing the straw, Intelisano looked puzzled.

"Was that there before?" Montalbano asked him.

"No, sir, it wasn't," said Intelisano. "The last time I come in here, about two or three months ago, there was nothin'. They brought it here."

He bent down and picked up a long piece of metal wire. He looked at it and passed it to the inspector.

"This is what you use to tie up bales of straw."

"Maybe they used the straw to sleep on," said Fazio.

Montalbano shook his head.

"No, I don't think they brought it here for sleeping," the inspector rebutted him. "They used it to hide something. If someone had happened to come up here and look inside through the damaged roof, all they would have seen was a pile of straw."

The floor was of beaten earth, untiled.

"Give me a hand removing some of this straw," Montalbano said to Fazio and Intelisano.

They pushed some of it aside, to the opposite side of the room.

Now they could see three broad streaks in the floor, one beside the other.

"These were made by three crates that were dragged along the ground," said Montalbano.

"They must have been pretty heavy," Fazio added.

"Maybe we ought to remove all the straw."

"All right. You go outside and smoke a cigarette, and I'll get Gallo and Signor Intelisano to help me," Fazio advised him.

"All right. But be careful and pay attention. Anything you see—I dunno, a piece of paper or metal—could be important and help us figure out who was in here."

"Gallo!" Fazio called.

Montalbano went outside and fired up a cigarette. Not knowing what to do to pass the time, he started walking and, without noticing, ended up behind the house. They'd left the board over the little window. Either they'd forgotten to remove it or it had seemed unimportant after they'd emptied the place out.

About thirty yards away stood eight or nine sickly almond trees that must have originally been part of some orchard rows long since gone.

There was nothing else around them. Or rather, there was only a desolate landscape quite similar to the one in his dream.

No, wait a second. Actually, if one looked closely, there were not eight or nine trees, but exactly fourteen.

Or, more precisely, there were nine whole trees with full trunk and foliage, and five trees with only the trunk remaining.

The upper parts had not been chopped off piece by piece with an axe. The trees looked as though they had been decapitated with a single blow, clean and precise, because each mane of leaves and branches lay on the ground, whole, some ten yards away from its respective trunk.

How could that have happened?

His curiosity aroused, he wanted to understand and went up to the nearest of the decapitated trees.

The cut was clean, as though made with a

scalpel. But he couldn't really get a good look, not even on tiptoe.

And so he took another ten steps and went and looked at a treetop that, in falling, had turned upside down.

No, it wasn't a sharp, powerful blade that had chopped the tree in a single cut, but something fiery. You could clearly see the dark brown signs where the wood had burned.

Suddenly he understood.

He turned on his heel and started running towards the house. As he rounded the corner he nearly collided with Fazio, who had come running to call him.

"What's going on?" Fazio asked.

"What's going on?" Montalbano asked at the same time.

"We found . . ." Fazio began.

"I found . . ." Montalbano began.

They stopped.

"Shall we conjugate all the tenses of the verb 'to find'?" Montalbano asked.

"You speak first," said Fazio.

"Behind the house I found some trees that had been cut with something that might have been a bazooka or a rocket launcher."

"Holy shit," said Fazio.

"And what did you want to tell me?"

"That we found six pages of the *Giornale dell'Isola*, all with oil stains."

"How much you want to bet that it was lubricant for weapons?"

"I never bet when I know I'll lose."

"There were weapons here, and the people wanted to test them by firing them at the trees. I'd bet the farm on it," said the inspector.

"So what do we do now?" asked Fazio.

"Quick, call the others."

"Where are we going?"

"Over to the trees to look for wood chips."

They combed the grass and the ground until one o'clock.

When they'd found about a kilo's worth of specimens, the inspector said it would suffice and they could go back to town.

They drove Intelisano home, advising him to remain available and not to talk about the matter with anyone. Then they headed back to headquarters.

"So what's the plan?" asked Fazio.

"Bring all the wood chips and newspaper pages into my office, then inform Mimì that we'll meet back up at four o'clock. I'm going to get in my car and go eat. Come to think of it, let me use your cell phone for a second."

He was afraid that, since it was already past two-thirty, Enzo might be closing. And he was so hungry he could hardly see.

"If I get there in fifteen minutes, can I still get something to eat?"

"It's closed!"

"This is Montalbano!"

It sounded like the desperate bark of a starving dog.

"Ah, sorry, Inspector, I didn't recognize you. Come whenever you like. For you we're always open."

Montalbano was walking through the station's parking lot, heading for his car, when he heard Catarella calling him.

"Chief! I gatta phone call f'yiz."

Good thing he'd called ahead to Enzo. He followed Catarella back to the switchboard.

"Chief, 'ere'd happen a be a lady onna line 'oo don't seem like much of a lady, an' she wants a talk t'yiz poissonally in poisson."

"Did she tell you her name?"

"She dinna wanna tell me, Chief. 'Ass why I said she din't seem like much of a lady."

"Explain what you mean."

"When I ast 'er the name o' the fimminine individdle in quession she jess started cussin'."

"What do you mean 'cussin'?"

"Cussin', Chief. She started takin' the Madonna's name in vain, sayin' Maria—"

Marian! The inspector snatched the receiver out of Catarella's hand, pressed the button for the line, then glared at his receptionist, who fled. When he tried to speak, his voice failed.

". . . ski?" was all he managed to say.

"Hi, Inspector, I'm at the airport. We're about to take off. I told you I'd call you this evening but I couldn't resist. I wanted to hear your voice."

Easier said than done! He still couldn't utter a single syllable.

"Well, at least wish me a pleasant journey."

"H-hav . . . a p-pleasant j-journey," he mouthed, feeling like he'd been handicapped since birth.

"I get it. You have people there and can't talk. Okay, ciao. I want you."

Montalbano set the receiver down and buried his face in his hands. If Catarella hadn't been in the vicinity, he would have started crying from shame.

5

They removed all the mail that was on his desk and piled it up higgledy-piggledy on the little sofa to make room for the wood chips and newspaper pages that they had stuffed into two bags, a jute sack for the chips and a plastic bag for the newspaper.

Montalbano locked the door to his office after telling Catarella not to disturb him for any phone calls or for any other reason, then sat down to consult with Augello and Fazio.

Seeing that neither of the two saw fit to open his mouth, the inspector prodded them.

"You guys do the talking."

He'd gone out to eat rather late and had been so hungry he couldn't hold back. For this reason, and because he'd been unable to take his walk along the jetty for lack of time, he now felt a bit muddled, despite downing three coffees. Not that he felt muddled or anything; he just didn't feel like talking.

"Well, in my opinion," Augello began, "they'll be back to use the house again. So I think we should set up some surveillance—not a twenty-four-hour watch, mind you, but we should have one of our men passing by often, even at night."

"I'm convinced instead that they won't be using the house again," said Fazio.

"Why's that?"

"Because, first of all, these kinds of improvised depots are always used only once and then abandoned, and, second, because Intelisano asked the two Tunisians working in his fields if they knew anything about the door. In short, the Tunisians were tipped off indirectly that Intelisano had discovered what was going on."

"So what? What makes you think the two Tunisians are complicit in the arms depot? Did a little bird tell you?"

"Nobody told me. But it's a possibility."

"Since when have you become a racist?" Augello pressed on provocatively.

Fazio didn't take offense.

"Dear Inspector Augello, you know perfectly well I'm not a racist. But I wonder how these weapons smugglers or terrorists—because that's what we're dealing with here, there's no getting around it—how did these people, who are certainly foreigners, come to know that there was a tumbledown house in a godforsaken spot that they could use? Somebody must have told them."

"I hate to admit it," said Augello, "but you're probably right. There's total chaos these days in Tunisia and they're desperately in need of weapons. So do you think we should arrest the two Tunisians and put the screws to them?"

"It seems to me the only logical thing to do."

"Just a second," Montalbano cut in, finally deciding to open his mouth. "I'm sorry, I've come to the conclusion that this investigation, for all its importance, is not for us to conduct."

"And why not?" Fazio and Augello resentfully asked in unison.

"Because we haven't got the means. It's as sure as death that there are fingerprints on those pages of newspaper. And it's as sure as taxes that there's someone somewhere capable of reading those wood chips and telling us what weapons were used and where they were made. And we don't have specialists like that. Is that clear? And therefore it's not up to us. Get over it. This is a job for the counterterrorism unit."

Silence ensued. Then Augello said:

"You're right."

"Good," said Montalbano. "So, since we're all in agreement, you, Mimì, gather all this stuff together—wood chips and newspaper—and take it to Montelusa. Ask for a meeting with Hizzoner the C'mishner, tell him everything, and then go, with his solemn blessing, to the counterterrorism department. After you've told them the whole story and turned over the bags, wish them a fond farewell and come back here."

Mimì looked doubtful.

"But wouldn't it be better if Fazio went, since

he was actually there when the newspaper and chips were found?"

"No, I would rather that Fazio got immediately down to work."

"Doing what?" asked Fazio.

"Go back to Intelisano and talk to him. Try to find out as much as you can about the two Tunisians. No one's saying we can't conduct a parallel investigation. But be careful: for the time being, nobody at the commissioner's office must know that we're moving on this too."

Fazio smiled in satisfaction.

Around seven o'clock, Catarella rang.

"Chief, 'ere'd be Pasquali 'oo'd be the son o' yer cleanin' lady Adelina 'oo says 'at if ya got the time 'e'd like to talk t'yiz poissonally in poisson."

"Is he on the line?"

"Nossir, 'e's onna premisses."

"Then send him in."

Pasquale doffed his cap as he entered.

"Good to see you, 'Spector."

"Hello, Pasqualì. Have a seat. Everything all right with the family?"

"Everything's fine, thanks."

"You got something for me?"

"Yeah. But first I need to know the exact time and place of the mugging. I think you said Vicolo Crispi, right?"

"Right. But wait just a second."

Montalbano got up, went into Fazio's room, grabbed the written report of di Marta's testimony, and wrote a telephone number down on a scrap of paper. Then he went back to his office, turned on the speakerphone, and dialed a number.

"I want you to hear this, too," he said to Pasquale.

"Hello?" said a young woman's voice.

"Inspector Montalbano here, police. I'd like to speak with Loredana di Marta."

"This is she."

"Good evening, signora. I'm sorry to bother you, but I need a little more information on the armed robbery of which you were the victim."

"Oh, God, no! I wouldn't want . . . I feel so . . ."

She seemed quite troubled.

"I know, signora, that you—"

"But didn't my husband tell you everything?"

"Yes, signora, but you were the person who was robbed, not your husband. Understand?"

"But what can I add to what he's already told you?"

"Signora, I realize that talking about this ugly incident is very painful for you. But you have to understand that I can't help but—"

"I'm sorry. I'll try to control myself. What is it you want to know?"

"Exactly how many nights ago did the attack take place?"

"Three."

"What time was it?"

"Well, purely by chance, right before I noticed the man lying on the ground and pulled over, I'd looked at the clock in the car. It was four minutes past midnight."

"Thank you for your courtesy and understanding. And now that you've told me when it happened, can you tell me where?"

"What? I think I've told you that over and over! In Vicolo Crispi, because I had to go and deposit—"

"Yes, I know, but where on Vicolo Crispi? Can you be more precise?"

"What do you mean, where?"

"Signora, Vicolo Crispi is not very long, right? I think I remember there's a bakery, a fabric sto—"

"Oh, I see. Just bear with me for a second. Okay. If I remember correctly . . . yes, that had to have been it, right between the fabric store and the Burgio jewelry shop. Just a few steps away from the night-deposit box."

"Thank you, Signora. For the moment I have nothing else to ask you."

He hung up and eyed Pasquale.

"Did you hear?"

"I heard."

"Was that what you wanted to know?"

"Yes."

71

"And so?"

"I can assure you the mugger's not part of the local action."

"So he's an outsider or a one-offer?"

"More likely a one-offer than an outsider."

"I see."

But Montalbano also saw that Pasquale had something else to say to him but couldn't make up his mind.

"Is there something else?"

"Maybe."

It was hard for him to say what he wanted to say.

"Speak. You know I'll never mention your name to anyone."

"I've never had any doubt of that, as far as that goes."

He made up his mind.

"It's all bullshit," said Pasquale.

"What's all bullshit?"

"What that lady just told you."

"How do you know?"

"Tell me something: Don't the police ever talk to the carabinieri? Or the carabinieri to the police?"

"Why do you ask?"

"Because Angelo Burgio, the jeweler with the shop in Vicolo Crispi, reported to the carabinieri that he'd been burglarized exactly three nights ago."

Montalbano's eyes opened wide.

"Can you tell me any more?"

"I could, but . . . don't forget what you said."

"There's nothing to worry about, Pasqualì."

"As they always do, the guys had posted a lookout inside the doorway to one of the buildings, where he could see all the way up and down the street. The lookout stayed there for a whole hour, from eleven-thirty to twelve-thirty. It don't add up."

"Meaning?"

"He didn't see anybody lying on the ground, and he didn't see any cars stop either."

"I see."

"And, for your information, I can also say that during that hour, the only vehicles that came down Vicolo Crispi were an ambulance, a small van, and a three-wheeler."

"Thanks, Pasqualì."

"Much obliged, Inspector."

And so the beautiful Loredana had told her husband a big fat lie.

They had to find out what really happened, and where the sixteen thousand euros had gone.

Every conjecture now became a possibility, starting with the chance that the mugging had taken place somewhere else, that Loredana had recognized the mugger and didn't have the courage to tell her husband, and ending with the possibility that Loredana was in cahoots with the mugger himself.

The inspector got up, went into Fazio's office, picked up the paper accompanying the report that Fazio had covered with notes, and there she was: Valeria Bonifacio, Loredana's bosom friend, Via Palermo 28. There was even her telephone number.

He sat down at Fazio's desk and dialed it.

"Hello?" said a woman at the other end.

Montalbano pinched his nose to change the sound of his voice.

"Is this the Bonifacio home?"

"Yes."

"I'm *ragioniere* Milipari of Fulconis Shipping. I'd like to speak with the captain."

"My husband is currently in Genoa. His ship called at port there."

"Okay, thanks. I'll call him on his cell. Oh, listen, if we want to send a package to him in Vigàta, will you be home tomorrow?"

"Yes, until ten a.m."

"Thank you, signora."

He hung up. He was determined to go and pay a visit to Signora Valeria early the next morning. With the husband not around to make trouble, it was more likely she would say what he wanted to know.

When he got home, he noticed that Adelina had left him a note on the kitchen table.

yissterday you et out an so I hed to trow out what I cookt wich was rilly a shem. An sints I see you hedda good campany lest nite, I didna mek nuthin for tonite, figgerin you was gonna eat out tonite too an thet way I woudna hev to trow out good food aggenn. If you wanna eat at hom tomorow leev me a note tellin me.

He cursed the saints. But this was not a vendetta on Adelina's part because a woman had slept there; indeed the housekeeper would roll out the red carpet for any eventual rival of Livia's, since she had a strong dislike of Livia, who repaid her fully in kind. No, Adelina's good faith was beyond dispute, but the fact remained that there was nothing to eat in the house.

It wasn't that he was really so hungry at that moment, but his appetite was liable to sneak up on him later.

Eating out again was out of the question. Marian was liable to call when he was out and he wouldn't be there to answer. He could, of course, take his cell phone with him, but he wouldn't have been able to speak in the presence of other people.

He opened the fridge. There was just a little jar of anchovies in olive oil.

But how could there not be anything else? Obviously Adelina had forgotten to restock him with the usual reserves of tumazzo and other cheeses, passuluna olives, salami . . .

He looked at his watch. In theory, there should have been enough time to go down to the Marinella Bar, buy a few provisions, and come back before Marian called.

He was halfway home when a tractor-trailer right in front of his car skidded and swerved crosswise, blocking the road. With a speed worthy of a race car driver in the Carrera Panamericana, he drove off the road, went about ten yards with two wheels on the slope of a ditch and the other two in the open countryside, at a tilt so sharp he looked exactly like a stuntman, then passed the semi and got back on the road.

He was immediately overcome by terror at what he had just done. His hands began to tremble. So he pulled over at the side of the road and waited until he was a little calmer and fit to drive again.

When he was just outside the front door of his house he heard the telephone ringing inside. Laden with shopping bags, he lost precious time searching for his keys and unlocking the door.

He shot inside, dropping the bags to the floor, and grabbed the receiver.

"Hello?"

He was greeted by a dial tone. Surely it had been Marian.

And now what? How could he have been so stupid not to have asked Marian for her cell phone number? Actually, to be more precise, he had no telephone number whatsoever for Marian, or even an address.

He had to resign himself.

After going and retrieving the shopping bags from the entranceway, he set the table on the veranda. But he still didn't feel like eating. He fired up a cigarette.

What was Marian doing in Milan at this hour?

The telephone rang. He raced over.

She was answering the question he'd just asked. As if by telepathy.

"Ciao, Inspector."

"Ciao. Was that you who called just a few minutes ago?"

"Yes. I'm just on my way out of my parents' house. I'm going to dinner with that dealer I mentioned. I've been speeding things up. I spent all afternoon glued to the telephone, because I want to get back as soon as possible. You have no idea how much I miss you."

She paused, then:

"If you don't have the courage to tell me anything else, tell me how much you like me."

"I like you . . . a lot."

"Can I call you later? Even if it's a little late?"

"Of course."

"I send you a kiss."

"Same . . ."

She stopped.

"Same who? You or someone else?"

"Me."

He hung up and headed out to the veranda on stiffened legs, but then the telephone rang again.

He figured Marian had forgotten to tell him something.

"Ciao, Salvo."

It wasn't Marian.

"Who is this?"

As he was asking the question, he realized he was making a mistake bigger than a skyscraper.

How could he not have recognized the voice at the other end? Perhaps because he still had Marian's voice ringing in his ears?

"Now that it's you who don't recognize my voice on the phone, what am I supposed to do?" Livia asked angrily.

There was no escaping it, he would have to start telling lies. He took a deep breath and dived in.

"Apparently you didn't realize I was kidding."

"I know you too well, Salvo. You were waiting for a call from another woman, I'm sure of it."

"Well, if you're so sure, then there's no point discussing the subject any further, is there?"

"Tell me her name."

Better to continue with the joke.

"Karol."

"Carol?!"

"Yes, what's so strange about that? Karol with a K. Exactly like the last pope, remember?"

"But is it a woman?"

"Of course."

He pretended to be offended.

"But how could you possibly imagine that I . . . with a man?"

"And what does she do?"

"She's a lap dancer in a club in Montelusa."

Livia thought about this for a minute. Then she said.

"I don't believe you. You're just fucking with me."

A tremendous weariness suddenly came over Montalbano.

He didn't have the courage to tell Livia what was happening to him. Not over the telephone. It would have been impossible.

"Listen, Livia, this is a very difficult moment for me, and—"

"At the office?"

He seized the escape valve.

"Yes, at the office. It's a long story that I'd like to tell you about in calmer circumstances and even ask for your advice, but very shortly Fazio's coming by to pick me up. I'll be back too late to call you. I'll call you tomorrow evening, if I can. All right?"

"All right," Livia said frostily.

The phone call had worn him out. He went back to the veranda and tried to eat something, but he just wasn't up to it.

He cleared the table and went and sat in the armchair in front of the television. He channel-surfed until he found a police film that went on for two hours, including the commercials. Then he watched the eleven o'clock news report on the Free Channel.

How was it that nobody said a thing about the burglary at Burgio Jewelers? Apparently the carabinieri had succeeded in keeping the news under wraps in order to conduct their investigation in peace.

He found a western that helped another two hours go by.

At last he turned off the set when his eyelids started drooping. Then he went out on the veranda and sat down.

This was a risky move, because it meant he would start thinking about his situation with Livia and Marian.

And he didn't want to do this. He wasn't ready yet.

Of course, sooner or later, he would have to face the matter head-on.

And whatever the solution turned out to be, it was certain to bring him much happiness and cause him great pain.

6

He glanced at his watch. Almost two. How long did dinners in Milan last, anyway? What the fuck! Not even if all the waiters were over eighty or walked on crutches could it take so long! And what did Marian and the dealer have to say to each other, after all? Did they have to review the entire history of art? True, she'd warned him she would call late, but here the birds were going to start chirping before long!

I'm going to unplug the phone and go to bed, he thought.

And at that exact moment the telephone rang.

He'd become so agitated in the previous few minutes that he gave a start in his chair that very nearly made him fall on the floor.

"He . . . hello!"

"Ciao, Inspector. Forgive me for keeping you waiting, but the dinner dragged on and on."

Montalbano the gentleman emerged in all his splendor.

"Forgive you? For what? I realize perfectly well that there are certain things . . ."

"And then Gianfranco wanted to go and have a drink in a nightclub. I got back just now."

Montalbano the gentleman was swallowed up by Montalbano the caveman.

"And who's this Gianfranco?"

"Gianfranco Lariani, the art dealer. Oh, that's right, I never told you his name. He was so insistent: 'Come on, what's it to you, five minutes—come on, don't be silly.' In short, I had to give in for diplomatic reasons."

Oh, how familiar they were with each other!

"Did you know him before?"

"Who, Gianfranco? No, but I think I already mentioned to you that it was Pedicini who told me to get in touch with him."

And so, right off the bat, on first meeting, they're all friendly and familiar, *come on, what's it to you, don't be silly* . . .

Better change the subject.

"Everything all right?"

"Everything's great. At least I think it is."

"Why do you say that?"

"Because Lariani's a slyboots, the kind that . . . doesn't bare his soul so easily."

And a good thing, too! That was all they needed! Montalbano couldn't hold back any longer.

"What's he like?"

"In what sense?"

"As a man."

"Well, very elegant, gentlemanly, around forty-five, rather good-looking . . ."

And there it was, the pang of jealousy kept long at bay, but in vain.

Zap! An arrow square in the chest.

"Did he try to seduce you?"

"I would have been surprised if he hadn't. You should have seen me! I was in top form. His jaw dropped when he saw me. But that's of no importance. I think Pedicini was right, and Lariani has the stuff."

"Did he tell you himself?"

"Not explicitly. But indirectly, he did. I told you he was a sly one, didn't I? He's not going to show his hand right away. But I realized he had a weakness. Money. In fact he opened up when I told him—without putting much emphasis on it— that I was in the habit of paying in ready cash, with bank transfers."

"So how did you leave things with him?"

"I'm going to go see him tomorrow afternoon."

Alarm bells started ringing.

"Where?" he asked, trying to seem indifferent.

"At his house."

No, no, no! This was getting serious!

"Why at his house, if I may ask? Doesn't this man have an office? Or is this the custom in Milan?"

"Don't be ridiculous, come on. From what I gathered, I think he has an apartment connected to his house where he keeps the paintings. But I doubt I'll conclude anything."

"Why not?"

"I know how these people operate. He'll show me a few daubs just to test me. I'll tell him I'm not interested in that kind of stuff, and he'll be forced to grant me another appointment. And that's when he'll let me into his inner sanctum."

"I don't understand."

"He'll show me his best stuff. And that'll be the moment to make a deal. Provided, of course, that Lariani, as I seem to have gathered, has what Pedicini is looking for."

"Why, what's he looking for?"

"Well, in seventeenth-century Italian painting, there are Madonnas, crucifixes, Nativities galore. But he's not interested in those subjects, or portraits either. What he wants is still lifes, landscapes, and genre scenes. And he wants large-format canvases."

"I see. But will this keep you away for a long time? Do you think you'll be able to conclude a deal soon?"

"I hope so. It's very hard being far away from you. It's never happened to me before, to feel so . . ."

She stopped.

"What did you do today?" she asked.

"At the office?"

"Yes. I want to share every minute of your life."

"Look, I'd be happy to tell you, but you'd just get bored."

"All right, I'll make it easier for you. Tell me what you did while waiting for my call."

"I watched two movies on TV and . . ."

He was about to say inadvertently that he'd spoken with Livia, but he held himself back just in time.

But Marian felt him braking.

"And?"

He didn't want to start telling lies to her too. One would be enough.

"Then Livia called."

"Oh."

A pause. Then:

"Did you tell her about us?"

"No."

"Why not?"

"I don't think it's the right time yet."

Another pause, longer this time.

"Look, Salvo, I hope you realize that for me, at least, this wasn't just a one-night stand. Nor is it just a momentary whim. I know myself too well."

"I realize that."

"And from what I felt the other night, I'm convinced it wasn't just a brief affair for you either."

"If I thought it was just a one-night stand, I wouldn't be here talking on the phone to you."

"We should talk about this together when I get back. But now I have to go. When I get into bed, I'm going to pretend you're lying there beside me. What time can I call you tomorrow?"

"I can't really say. Why don't we just get in

touch in the evening, when we'll have more time to talk?"

"Whatever you say. Good night, my dear Inspector."

There were two options. Clear and precise. Either stay up thinking about how to broach the question with Livia, or try to fall asleep immediately, with the sound of Marian's voice still in his ears.

He chose the second, closing his eyes and forcing himself to sleep.

The amazing thing was that he succeeded.

His last thought was a question: How long had it been since he'd spoken with Livia that way?

He woke up feeling satisfied. It was a beautiful day. He drank a mug of coffee, took a shower, shaved, and, before going out, wrote a note to Adelina informing her he'd be eating at home that evening.

He got in his car at eight-thirty and by nine-twenty was parking in Via Palermo, right in front of number 28.

It took him that long because Via Palermo was in the elevated part of Vigàta, the outermost suburb on the edge of the countryside, and consisted of many small, freestanding houses fairly distant from one another, each surrounded by a yard. The house at number 28 looked well tended. The little iron gate in front was open.

He went through the gate, walked up the little path, and rang the buzzer.

"Who is it?" a woman asked a few seconds later.

"Inspector Montalbano, police."

A pause.

"Who are you looking for?"

"Signora Valeria Bonifacio."

More silence. Then the voice said:

"I'm here alone."

What, was he a rapist or something?

"Signora, I repeat, I'm—"

"Okay, but I haven't got dressed yet."

"I can wait."

"Couldn't you come back this afternoon?"

"No, signora, I'm sorry."

"Then I'll let you in in about ten minutes."

His method of never letting the person know in advance that he was coming always worked.

Surely at that very moment Valeria was picking up the phone to talk to her friend Loredana and find out how she should act.

He smoked a cigarette. Via Palermo had little traffic, especially since there were no shops. During the ten minutes that he waited, only one car passed.

He went back and rang the buzzer again.

"Inspector Montalbano?"

"Yes."

The lock clicked, and the inspector pushed the door in and entered.

Signora Valeria came forward to greet him, hand extended, then led him into the living room and sat him down in an armchair.

For whatever reason, Montalbano had expected a middle-aged woman, whereas Valeria was quite young, probably the same age as Loredana, blond and pretty, with a shapely figure put duly on display by a form-fitting blouse and tight pants.

"Would you like a cup of coffee?"

"Thanks, but no."

She sat down in another armchair opposite his and crossed her legs. She looked at him and smiled. But Montalbano could tell that the smile was a bit tense. She was clearly on tenterhooks but controlled herself well.

"What can I do for you, Inspector?"

"I'm truly sorry for disturbing you. Didn't someone call you from the station to inform you of my visit?"

"No, nobody told me anything."

"Well, they'll hear from me when I get back to the office. I need some information from you concerning the armed robbery of your friend Loredana di Marta. You must know that—"

"Yes, I know the whole story. Loredana told me over the phone. She was in shock. I went immediately to see her and she told me everything, even . . . the disgusting details."

"Are you referring to the kiss?"

"Not only."

Montalbano got worried.

Want to bet that Signor di Marta had only sung half the mass? And the whole incident was more serious?

"Were there other things?"

"Yes."

"Could you be clearer?"

"It disgusts me to talk about it. To make a long story short, he grabbed her by the hand and put it . . . understand?"

"Yes. Did he go any further?"

"Luckily, no. But Loredana says the whole experience was disgusting, horrible."

"She's absolutely right. Well, at least it ended there. Do you remember at what time your friend left here that evening?"

"I couldn't really say exactly."

"Roughly, then."

"Well, it must have been a little before midnight, because the clock chimed after Loredana left."

She gestured towards a huge pendulum clock, of the kind that functions as furniture, in a corner of the large living room.

"Nice," said the inspector.

Even if it wasn't precise, since it was a few minutes fast.

"Yes. It was my father's. He had a mania for pendulum clocks. Our house was full of them. I managed to break free and kept only that one."

"So shall we say that it was around ten minutes to twelve?"

"Maybe a quarter to."

"Not more?"

"I really don't think so."

"Signora, it's essential for us to know as precisely as possible the time at which the robbery took place."

"Then I can confirm: quarter to twelve."

"Thank you. Does Loredana always leave so late?"

"No. Normally she leaves before dinnertime."

"So that evening was an exception."

"Yes."

"May I ask why?"

"I wasn't feeling well and Loredana didn't want to leave me. She was very worried, but it turned out to be just a passing malaise."

"Do you live alone? Aren't you married?"

"Yes, I am. But my husband's a captain of a container ship and stays away for long periods of time."

"I see. But, tell me something. Was Loredana still here when she realized she had forgotten to make the deposit for her husband? Or, as far as you know, did it only dawn on her after she left?"

"No, she remembered as soon as she got here. In fact, she wanted to go right back out and take care of it. It was I who told her she could do it later. I had to insist a little."

"Ah, so it was you?"

"Yes. And I felt terribly guilty afterwards for what happened. If I'd just let her go when she wanted to . . ."

"Come now, signora! What are you thinking? It was just an unexpected coincidence!"

He stood up.

"You've been very helpful, signora. Thank you."

"I'll show you out," said Valeria.

Just as she was opening the door, Montalbano asked:

"Do you know Carmelo Savastano?"

He hadn't foreseen the effect of his words. Valeria turned pale and took a step backwards.

"Why . . . do . . . you . . . ask?"

"Well, since I found out that your friend Loredana had been in a long relationship with this Savastano . . ."

"But what's that got to do with the robbery?"

She'd raised her voice without realizing it.

"Nothing at all, signora. I'm just curious."

By now Valeria had recovered.

"Of course I know him. Loredana and I have always been friends. But I haven't seen Carmelo for a long time."

While getting in the car, he glanced at his watch. Ten-thirty-one. He drove off.

But instead of heading for the office, he went in

the direction of Vicolo Crispi, trying to drive fast. The traffic was normal.

When he got to Vicolo Crispi, between the fabric shop and Burgio Jewelers, he looked at his watch again. Eleven past eleven. It had taken him forty minutes.

Based on what Valeria and Loredana had said, it had taken the girl only nineteen minutes to cover the same distance. Not counting the fact that Valeria's clock was fast. At that time, however, it was almost midnight, and therefore you had to take into account that there was a lot less traffic.

As soon as he sat down at his desk, he wanted confirmation and phoned Loredana.

"Montalbano here."

"Again?"

"Sorry, but I have only one question."

"Oh, all right."

"Do you remember precisely what time it was when you left your friend Valeria Bonifacio's house on the evening of—"

"It was quarter to twelve."

Lightning fast, without the slightest hesitation.

Apparently just after he left, Valeria had filled Loredana in on their conversation.

He called Fazio.

"Got any news for me?"

"A couple of things."

"Me too."

"Then you go first, Chief."

Montalbano told him what he'd learned from Pasquale; Fazio, in any case, knew how things stood with Adelina's son. Then the inspector told him about his meeting with Valeria Bonifacio, ending with the call he'd just made to Loredana.

"Sorry, Chief," said Fazio, "but if we know with some certainty that Signora di Marta's car did not drive down Vicolo Crispi that night, why are you so interested in knowing how much time it took the girl to get there from Via Palermo?"

"Think about it for a minute. Can I possibly write in the report that I know that her car never drove down Vicolo Crispi because I spoke with a thief who spoke with the lookout for a band of burglars? Can I have Pasquale and the lookout called as witnesses? No."

"You're right."

"And, even if I could pull off the miracle of calling them as witnesses, no one would believe a word they say. The defense lawyer would rip them to shreds. Because they're thieves known to law enforcement and therefore branded as liars by nature. Whereas a great many thieves not known to law enforcement can tell all the lies they want and everyone will believe them, because they're lawyers, politicians, economists, bankers, and so on. And so we have to prove, playing by the rules, that Loredana is not telling the truth."

"And how will we do that?"

"In the meantime I want you to do me a favor."

"Anytime."

"Tonight, starting at quarter to midnight, I want you to drive your car from Via Palermo to Vicolo Crispi. Then tomorrow morning you can tell me how long it took you."

"Wouldn't it be better to send Gallo instead?"

"No, because it would only take him seven-and-a-half minutes, if that. And now you talk."

"I went and talked with Intelisano, and he gave me the names and address of the two Tunisians, who live in Montelusa. They're both about fifty years old and good workers, and all their papers are in order because they were granted political asylum after arriving illegally four years ago."

Montalbano pricked up his ears.

"Political asylum?"

"Yessirree."

"We need to find out how they were able to prove—"

"Already taken care of."

Whenever Fazio said that, it irritated Montalbano.

"Then if you've already taken care of it, please be so kind as to fill me in."

Fazio took notice.

"Sorry, Chief, but I thought—"

"No, I'm the one who's sorry," said the inspector, immediately regretting his pique. "Go on."

"They both have sons in jail. Antigovernment

activities. There were arrest warrants out for the fathers, too, but they were able to escape in time."

Montalbano twisted up his mouth.

"These two Tunisians smell a little fishy to me."

7

"Good morning, everyone," Mimì Augello said upon entering.

"Congratulations," replied the inspector, smiling. "You were right."

Mimì acted astonished.

"Congratulations? And you actually admit I'm right? What on earth is happening? What is this, world kindness day? And what is it you think I'm right about?"

"The two Tunisians."

"Meaning?"

"They're political refugees. Enemies of the Tunisian government. They've both got sons in jail back home. So it's likely that—"

"Stop!" Augello cried. "Nobody move!"

"What is going on?" asked Montalbano.

"I hereby inform you all that we have been officially taken off the case by the commissioner. He said to me, and I quote: 'Tell Montalbano that as of this moment the investigation is in the hands of the counterterrorism unit. And that he mustn't interfere, or there'll be trouble.' There, you've been informed. And now, with all best wishes to the commissioner, how shall we proceed with the Tunisians?"

"As things stand now, I haven't the slightest

idea," the inspector admitted. "But something might come to me after I eat. Fazio, tell Inspector Augello the business about the mugging of Signora di Marta."

When Fazio had finished telling him the whole story, Mimì looked questioningly at Montalbano.

"And what do *you* think about all this?"

"Mimì, I put myself in the mugger's shoes. Assuming Loredana's story is true, which we know is not the case. So there I am, waiting in a doorway in Vicolo Crispi for a car to pass, so I can throw myself down on the ground. Now, as the thief, I have no idea what's inside that coming car. Imagine there's two or three men inside. Already, even if I'm armed, the whole business becomes more complicated. Because one of the guys is gonna get out of the car and check out the situation, while the other or others wait inside the car, ready to react however they want. And what if meanwhile another car passes? No, it's just too risky. Unless you know from the start what car is going to come down the street, and especially who's going to be in it."

"In conclusion?"

"In conclusion, the mugging, if there was indeed a mugging, must have happened somewhere else and in other circumstances, and the mugger must have had at least one accomplice."

"I agree," said Mimì. "But the question now is where do we go from here? We're certain the lady's telling us lies, but how do we get her to admit it?"

"We'll get her to give us some clues without her knowing. We'll call her into the station this afternoon, let's say at four-thirty. Fazio, take care of it and get back to me with a confirmation. If she wants to bring her husband along, there's no problem. I'll ask her a few questions, and afterwards we'll decide how to proceed. But you, Mimì, mustn't show your face anywhere around here for any reason whatsoever when Signora di Marta is here."

Mimì made a resentful face.

"And why can't I be present for this meeting?"

"I'll explain later, after she's gone. It's better for you, believe me. You have everything to gain from it."

As he was heading out to the end of the jetty, it occurred to him that if he had a clear idea of how to act with Loredana di Marta, he had no idea how to approach the two Tunisians.

He had to go about it carefully, because if it became known that they were under investigation, the immigration authorities might send them straight back to Tunisia without a second thought, without considering that they might be sending them to be tortured or killed. How many other times had they done the same with other poor bastards who'd met a nasty end after they'd been repatriated? He didn't want to have this on his conscience.

When he sat down on the flat rock, he noticed at once that the crab was waiting there for him.

"Greetings," he said.

He reached down, picked up a handful of pebbles, got rid of the bigger stones, and the game began. It consisted of tossing tiny pebbles at the crab. If he missed, the crab would remain motionless. If he hit it, the crab would move a few centimeters sideways. Until, finally, it arrived at the water's edge and vanished.

As he was watching it move laterally, Montalbano realized that the way to approach the two Tunisians was to move exactly the way the crab did: sideways.

In the twinkling of an eye he came up with a precise plan that would bring no harm to the two Arabs.

To reward himself, he decided to smoke one more cigarette, after which he returned to the office.

Where he called Fazio straight away and told him to come and listen to the telephone call he was about to make to Intelisano.

"Hello, Montalbano here. Sorry to bother you, but I urgently need to talk to you."

"When?"

"By this evening, if possible."

Intelisano thought about this for a moment.

99

"Would seven o'clock be too late?"

"No, that's perfect."

He hung up.

"What do you want from him?"

"Didn't I tell you that after lunch a good idea would come to me?"

"So what is it?"

"To go with Intelisano tomorrow morning to the Spiritu Santo district and have him introduce me to the two Tunisians under a false name with no mention of course that I'm with the police. I'll have him say I'm interested in buying the land. Do you like it so far?"

"Yeah. Then what?"

"Then in the afternoon I'll go back there, alone this time, and tell the two Tunisians that Intelisano mustn't find out about this visit because I want to hear the truth about that land from them. How productive it is, how much it earns, and so on. And I'll also ask about the barren part, where the little house is, since Intelisano is selling the whole property as a unit. Naturally, I'll pay them well. And since one thing leads to another, I'm hoping to extract some useful information."

"Sounds to me like a good idea," said Fazio.

Mimì Augello came in.

"How much time do I have before I disappear?"

Montalbano looked at his watch.

"About five minutes."

"I wanted to tell you that I just remembered

something. This Loredana, was she a checkout girl at the supermarket in Via Libertà before marrying di Marta?"

Fazio answered for Montalbano.

"She sure was."

"Then we know each other."

"*O matre santa!*" Montalbano exclaimed. "You mean you—"

"No, but a friend of mine tried, and I met her through him. Then this friend gave up on her because she'd long been with some guy she was hopelessly in love with."

"So she knows you're with the police?"

"No. I introduced myself as the lawyer Diego Croma."

Montalbano started laughing. It sounded to him like a character in a Harlequin romance.

"So that was your nom de guerre?"

"One of many."

"Tell me another. This is fun."

"Carlo Alberto de Magister. But that was when I was playing the gent with noble blood. But will the fact that we know each other compromise what you've got in mind?"

"No. On the contrary."

The telephone rang.

"Chief, 'ere'd be a male jinnelman an' a female lady onna premisses sayin' you summonsed 'em 'ere."

"Is it Mr. and Mrs. di Marta?"

"I dunno if 'ere bote called Martha, Chief, but one of 'em's a man an' th'other's a lady."

Montalbano got discouraged.

"Never mind, Cat. Just—"

"Bu' if you like, Chief, I c'n ask e'm fer their peculiars."

"I said never mind. Tell you what: Count up to ten, then bring them in here to me."

"Shou' I count ou' loud, Chief?"

"Count however you like, Cat."

He hung up.

"I'm outta here," said Mimì, opening the door and leaving.

"Leave it open!" Montalbano shouted to him.

A minute went by, and still no sign of anybody.

"How long's it take Catarella to count to ten anyway?" Fazio asked.

Another half minute later, Montalbano picked up the phone.

"Well, Cat?"

"Ya gotta 'ave patience, Chief, 'cuz nobuddy's lettin' me finish countin' a ten—one minnit iss the phone, next minnit iss summon cummin' up to me, an' so I gotta stop countin' an' start all over, an' now 'at you called me too, I forgot 'ow far I got an' I gotta start all over again again."

"Stop counting and just bring them in."

Moments later he saw, at the back of the corridor, Signor di Marta and his wife coming towards his office. He stood up and went out to greet them, introduced himself to the wife, and led them inside and sat them down in front of his desk.

Fazio settled into the chair in front of the computer.

Loredana di Marta, who wasn't quite twenty-one but looked eighteen, was a genuine dark beauty. Tall with long legs and eyes that must have been luminous but were now a bit clouded with emotion, which also made her nervous and pale.

Instinctively the inspector's eyes fell on her plump lips. They were perfect in outline, with no trace of her assailant's bite.

"We came here without any questions, but I have to say I don't understand the reason for . . ." di Marta immediately began.

Montalbano's raised hand silenced him.

"Signor di Marta, just remember that if you are present here at this discussion, as you requested, it is only because I've granted you this courtesy. You therefore mustn't intervene in any way, is that clear? You will best understand the reason for this meeting by listening in silence to the questions I ask your wife."

"All right," di Marta muttered.

"I'll try to keep you here as briefly as possible," Montalbano said to the girl. "So without any further ado, I'll get straight to the questions. Please tell me at what point of the evening your husband gave you the money to deposit."

Husband and wife exchanged a quick glance. Clearly they hadn't expected the inspector to begin with that question.

"When I was on my way out to see my friend Valeria."

"And what time was that?"

"Probably around eight-thirty."

"And you hadn't had any other opportunity to visit your friend during the day?"

"I'd already been to her place in the afternoon, from four-thirty to seven."

"And after dinner you felt the need to go back there?"

"Yes. She wasn't feeling well. I went home at seven, as I said, and made dinner for my husband. Then after we ate I told him I had to go out again, and that was when he gave me the money to deposit."

"Was it the first time?"

"Was what the first time?"

"That it was you depositing the money instead of him."

"No, I'd done it before."

"I see. But on the way to your friend's house you forgot about it."

"Yes. I was thinking of other things. I was . . . I was so worried about Valeria."

"That's understandable. So therefore there were only three people who knew that you had that money in your purse."

"Two people," Loredana corrected him. "My husband and me."

"No," said Montalbano. "Valeria Bonifacio told me that as soon as you, Signora di Marta, got to her place you remembered that you were supposed to have deposited that cash and that you even wanted to go back out to do it, but your friend talked you out of it, saying you could do it on your way home. Is that correct?"

"Yes, that's correct."

"So, as you see, I was right. There were three of you who knew about it. Do you rule out the possibility that anyone else could have known?"

"Yes, I would rule that out completely."

"You didn't stop anywhere on your way to your friend's house?"

"Why would I have stopped anywhere?"

"It happens, signora. Maybe you'd run out of cigarettes and needed to buy more, something like that."

"But I don't see how that could have anything—"

"I'll tell you why I asked. Because if you did stop to buy something, it's possible that somebody noticed that you had a lot of money in your purse."

"I didn't stop anywhere."

Montalbano paused and decided that it was time for amateur hour—time, that is, for a little theater.

He screwed up his lips in a grimace, whistled,

stared for a long time in silence at a ballpoint pen, and finally started wailing softly:

"Ahh! Ahh!"

Di Marta looked at him in dismay but didn't say a word. Loredana, however, spoke:

"What is the meaning of this?"

"It means it doesn't look good."

"For whom?" the girl asked angrily.

"What a question, signora! Can't you figure it out for yourself?"

"No, I can't!"

"For your friend, Valeria, signora! It's obvious!"

"What are you saying?" Loredana said, confused.

"My dear signora, allow me to formulate a hypothesis. Just a hypothesis, mind you. You arrive at your friend's place saying you forgot to deposit a huge sum of money and would like to go back out and do it at once, but your friend talks you out of it. Don't you find that strange?"

"Why do you find it so strange? Given the fact that sooner or later I was going to go back home . . ."

"No, no, no. It's one thing for you to go and make the deposit at nine p.m., and it's another thing altogether for you to go and do it at midnight. And alone. A woman as young and—if I may say so—as beautiful as you! Don't you think it was a rather careless suggestion, to say the least?"

"But I had no idea I would be staying so long at Valeria's, and she didn't either!"

The girl was quick with her answers, no doubt about it.

"Let me continue with my hypothesis. Your friend purposely exaggerated her malaise to force you to stay late. And so, as soon as you leave her place, she rushes to the telephone to call her accomplice, informing him that you'll be passing through Vicolo Crispi with a large sum of money in your purse. So the guy races there and sets up the scam."

Loredana was glaring at him in astonishment, mouth wide open. The inspector made a gesture as if waving away a fly.

"But let's set aside that argument, which concerns our investigation of Signora Bonifacio. And I ask that neither of you make any mention of these suspicions of mine to her. But let's move on to the next question. You say that between the fabric store and Burgio Jewelers in Vicolo Crispi you saw a man on the ground. My question is this—and you should think carefully before answering: That man, when you first noticed him, was he already on the ground or in the process of falling to the ground?"

"What difference does it make?"

"It makes a huge difference."

"I don't understand."

"I'll explain. Now pay attention. Your attacker

certainly did not lie down on the ground in order to rob the first car to drive by. What if it was a truck or a three-wheeler? What's he going to rob from them? Five euros? No, he has to wait for the right car to pass. And so he stays hidden in a doorway, and as soon as he sees your car coming, he throws himself down on the ground. Do you follow?"

"Yes."

"But since Vicolo Crispi is not very long and perfectly straight, you must have seen not a man already fallen but a man in the process of falling. Is this all clear to you?"

She looked him straight in the eye. Now her gaze was no longer clouded; it was sharp and alive. She apparently was a rather intelligent girl. She was proving to be a formidable opponent.

"I stand by my declaration," Loredana said firmly. "It's possible I didn't notice the man moving because I was looking at the clock or doing something else, but when I saw him, the man was already lying on the ground."

Hats off. She wasn't just smart, but shrewd. She'd understood that by reconfirming her version of events, she was weakening the inspector's hypothesis as to Valeria's complicity. Montalbano sensed that his next question might trigger a row. And so he coolly decided to spring it on her by surprise, to achieve maximum effect.

"I'm sorry, but in your statement it says that as

soon as he got in the car, the attacker took the keys out of the ignition and threw them into the street."

"That's right."

"So after your attacker left, you had to get out of the car and look for them?"

"That's right."

"Did it take you very long?"

"I think so. The street's not very well lit, and I was upset."

"Which way did he go?"

"He started running in the direction my car was pointed in, with the headlights shining on his back. Then at the bottom of the street he turned right."

"Moving on," said Montalbano, "your friend Valeria also mentioned a detail to me that curiously does not figure in the report filed by your husband."

Signor di Marta, who up until that moment had been listening attentively, made an ugly face and butted in.

"I told you everything!"

"You told us everything your wife told you," Montalbano clarified.

Di Marta understood immediately. He turned angrily towards Loredana. He looked like an infuriated bull ready to gore.

"Didn't you tell me everything? What else happened? And yet you swore you'd told me everything!"

The girl didn't answer, but only kept her eyes lowered. Montalbano realized he should intervene.

"I told you you mustn't—"

"I'll talk whenever I bloody well please!"

"Fazio, accompany Signor di Marta out of this office," the inspector said coldly.

"What is the meaning of this?" the other reacted, jumping to his feet.

"It means I consider your presence no longer convenient at this time."

"This is an outrage! An abuse of power!" di Marta yelled, pale as a corpse and clenching his fists.

But Fazio had grabbed him forcefully by the shoulders and was pushing him outside as he kept on yelling.

"Would you like some water?" the inspector asked the girl.

She nodded yes. Montalbano got up, grabbed a glass, filled it from the bottle he normally kept on top of the filing cabinet, and handed it to her.

She drank it down in a single gulp.

Fazio returned.

"I persuaded him to wait in the waiting room. At any rate, I've got someone keeping an eye on him."

"Do you feel up to continuing?" Montalbano asked.

"Well, I'm here," she said, resigned.

"Why didn't you tell your husband that the

robber, on top of the kiss, had demanded something else?"

Loredana turned flaming red. Her upper lip was damp with sweat. She was forcing herself with visible effort to remain calm, but it was clear she was very upset.

"Because . . . he's very jealous. Sometimes he's quite irrational. He gets so blind with jealousy he's liable to say I consented. Anyway, I thought that if I told him . . . something bad might happen to him, physically. I wanted to spare him . . . And I honestly don't understand why Valeria felt obliged to go and tell you . . ."

"Your friend acted correctly. But to be honest with you, I was under the impression she didn't tell me everything."

It was a shot in the dark. He hadn't had that impression at all. It was Loredana's agitation that had given him the idea.

8

Loredana didn't answer. Indeed, she seemed not even to have heard the inspector. She was staring hard at the floor, shoulders slightly hunched. Every so often she would shake her head as if to discard some troubling thought or memory. Then she opened her handbag, extracted a small embroidered handkerchief, and wiped her upper lip. When she'd finished, she held it tightly with both hands.

The inspector figured that this was the right moment to throw down his trump card. He closed his eyes, reopened them, and fired away.

"Would you please give me the name and address of your gynecologist?"

Loredana gave a start in her seat. She turned and looked at Montalbano with surprise and fear.

"Why?"

She'd shouted it out, with all her heart, goggling her eyes and stiffening all over, nerves tensed.

Montalbano couldn't help but congratulate himself. He'd been right on target.

"Because I want to ask him a question that he'll have to answer, since it won't violate any norms of professional secrecy."

"What question?"

Loredana's voice was barely audible.

"I will ask him, quite simply, when was the last time you went in to him for an examination."

Loredana suddenly started crying in despair. Remaining seated, she turned three-quarters towards him, sliding to the edge of the chair. Then she joined her hands in supplication and laid them on the desk.

"For heaven's sake . . . stop! Take pity on . . ."

Fazio was staring at him, but Montalbano avoided his gaze.

"I'm sorry, signora, but I have no choice but to continue. Try to control yourself. Do it for your husband's sake. If he sees you so upset . . . I'll help you out, okay?"

"How?"

"I'll tell you what I think happened, and if I get anything wrong, I want you to correct me. So. The attacker made you get into the car, took the money from your purse and then, threatening you with a gun, ordered you to start the car. Is that right?"

Loredana nodded yes. She was now holding the handkerchief up against her face with both hands, almost as if she didn't want to see the world around her.

"Then, as soon as you were in a dark, secluded spot, he told you to pull over and get into the backseat. Am I right?"

"Yes."

"And then he raped you."

"Yes," said Loredana, almost voicelessly.

113

Then, with a cry, she fainted, sliding off the chair and to the floor.

Rushing to her aid, Montalbano and Fazio collided. Then Fazio lifted her bodily and laid her down on the little sofa. Montalbano wiped her face with his handkerchief, which he had wet with water from the bottle. It took them about ten minutes to rouse her.

"Do you feel like taking a few steps?"

"Yes."

"Fazio, take the young lady into your office and stay there with her."

The moment they left, he rang Catarella.

"Bring the gentleman in the waiting room into my office."

"Where is my wife?" di Marta asked as soon as he entered and didn't find her there.

"She's in Fazio's office. As soon as your wife pulls herself together, he's going to draft her new deposition."

"*New* deposition?!"

They stared at each other. There was no need for the inspector to say anything else. Di Marta seemed suddenly short of breath. And his head began to shake, quake. He brought a hand to his heart. Montalbano feared he might have an attack.

All they needed was for him to faint too.

"She was raped, wasn't she?"

"Unfortunately," said Montalbano.

• • •

Five minutes after the di Martas left, the inspector held a conference with Fazio and Mimì. First off, Montalbano told Fazio to bring Augello up to speed on the investigation while he went out to the parking lot to smoke a cigarette.

He needed to think alone about what had just happened. When he returned, he opened the session.

"I want to hear from you first, Fazio. Do you have any questions for me?"

"I do. I realized when you expressed your supposed suspicions of La Bonifacio, that it was only to provoke the reaction that Valeria will have as soon as Loredana tells her about it. But, concerning what happened after the kiss, were you really under the impression that Bonifacio, when she mentioned the fondling, hadn't told you the whole story?"

"No. At the time, when I was talking to her, I didn't have that impression. It was Loredana's attitude here, with us, that led me to realize what her game was."

"Sorry, but what game do you mean?"

"Didn't you think Loredana wanted to take me by the hand and lead me wherever she wanted to go? And like a good boy I held out my hand for her and let myself be led?"

"Are you trying to tell me she *wasn't* raped?" Mimì asked. "Then what was her reason for going in for medical examination?"

115

"That's not what I'm saying. I'm saying that she let herself be raped. She needed certification of a sexual attack. And got it from her gynecologist. Please note that she didn't tell us of her own accord that she'd been raped; she made me force it out of her. She's extremely clever."

"But for what purpose?"

"I'll tell you for what purpose. Clearly, though, those two women . . . So Loredana comes home with a bite on her lips. Valeria tells me the mugger also had her touch him, and then Loredana comes here all agitated as if she's hiding something . . . How skillfully those two managed to plant the idea in my head that she'd been raped! They worked together perfectly! A couple of real pros, those two!"

"All right," Augello said impatiently. "But what need was there for her to have been raped?"

"To neutralize any suspicion of complicity between her and the mugger."

"You're right," Fazio quickly chimed in.

"And for that reason, since two plus two usually equals four, the rapist and rape victim must have been in cahoots, which means that Loredana can lead us to the mugger. And this, Mimì, is where you come in."

"I get it. You want me to come on to Loredana."

"You're wrong."

"So what am I supposed to do then?"

"Come on to Valeria Bonifacio. Who, I assure

you, is worth the effort, as women go. Have Fazio fill you in on everything, and don't set foot back here until you've established contact with her."

Montalbano noticed that Fazio looked pensive.

"What is it?"

"I'm not convinced, Chief."

"You're not in agreement over Inspector Augello's assignment?"

"That's fine. I'm not convinced they would go through this whole song and dance for just sixteen thousand euros."

"Why, does that seem like so little to you?"

"It's plenty, but it doesn't seem like a lot in relation to all the rest. But that's just my impression."

"You may be right. But given where we stand, we have no choice but to move forward."

There was a pause, and then he continued.

"Anyway, I have a vague idea myself as to the identity of this mugger, which came to me the moment I realized we were dealing with a consensual encounter."

"As far as that goes," said Fazio, "I've got an idea myself."

"Oh, yeah? Then tell me the name."

"You tell me."

"Tell you what. I'll say his first name, and you say his last. Okay?"

"Okay."

"Carmelo . . ." the inspector began.

"Savastano," Fazio concluded.

"Wow, what a couple of geniuses you are!" Mimì exclaimed in disdain. "It was so obvious it was him that I didn't even want to take part in your silly competition, which seemed like something out of kindergarten."

He got up and left. The telephone rang.

"Chief, 'ere'd be a Signor Intelligiano onna premisses."

"Is he intelligent?"

"I dunno, Chief, wan' me to ax 'im?"

"No, just send him in."

Intelisano had no problem with doing what Montalbano asked of him.

"That's fine with me, Inspector. If you wanna go an' talk to the two Tunisians in Spiritu Santo, it's more convenient to go by way of Montelusa, 'cause there's a good road there. That's what I always do."

"So what's the plan?"

"I think it's best if we go in two cars, mine and yours. We can meet outside Montelusa, at the intersection for Aragona. Seven-thirty okay with you?"

"Seven-thirty sounds perfect."

"How should I introduce you?"

"As Engineer Carlo La Porta."

He was about to head home when Catarella rang to tell him that Dr. Squisito from Counterterrorism was on the premises and wanted to talk to him personally in person.

"His name is Sposìto, Cat. Send him in."

Sposìto was an assistant commissioner of about forty-five, always shabbily dressed and disheveled and always in a hurry. He and the inspector had never had any direct dealings with each other, but had crossed paths many times at Montelusa Central, and Montalbano found him reasonably likable.

"I'll take just five minutes of your time," said Sposìto. "I'm in a hurry. Since I was already coming this way, I thought I'd take advantage of—"

"No problem at all. Have a seat."

"I'll start by saying that we've already checked out the little house in Spiritu Santo—on the sly, of course—and you were absolutely right. It was almost certainly being used as a depot for one crate of rocket launchers and two crates of ammunition. But I need some further clarification."

"I'm glad to help. What do you need to know?"

"According to what Inspector Augello told us, when the property's owner noticed that a door had been put on the house, he didn't come to report this to you the same day that he discovered it, but the following day. Is that right?"

"No, he came the evening of the same day, but I'd already left and Augello told him to come back the following day."

"And did you go to the site on the very morning the report was made?"

"Yes. Why do you ask?"

"Because if that's the case, it's clear that someone's been keeping an eye on the house—someone who knew that Intelisano wasn't just some passerby, but the owner. And they must have immediately taken measures and rushed over there to empty it out as soon as Intelisano went away."

"I see. And so?"

"And so it's possible—since for them it was an unexpected surprise—that the weapons haven't yet been sent away to their destination. They may have been moved somewhere close by, perhaps not far from the house, maybe even in a place that wouldn't be too hard to find. So there you have it. Thanks."

He got up, they shook hands.

How come Sposìto didn't say a word about the two Tunisians? Was it possible he hadn't yet been informed of them? Or did he not want to talk about them with him?

When the inspector got home, the first thing he did was to make sure that Adelina hadn't left him to starve despite the note he'd left for her.

He found a savory cake of potatoes and anchovies in the oven. A big one. Apparently Adelina, not knowing whether he would be alone, decided to make enough for two and more.

He'd just finished setting the table on the veranda when the telephone rang.

"Ciao, Inspector."

"Ciao, Marian. How'd it go with Lariani?"

That was what he was keenest to know.

"Badly."

He grew alarmed. Want to bet the bastard had invited her to his house just to take advantage of her?

"Did he touch you?"

"Come on, are you kidding? Do you really think I would have let him? No, it went badly because, as I'd expected, he showed me some second-rate stuff, and when I told him to stop kidding around, he replied that he might be able to get me what I was looking for, but he would need more time and would have to give it some thought."

"How much time?"

"At least two days."

"He's really dragging it out."

"Yes he is. Which means unfortunately that I won't be able to return to Vigàta as soon as I'd hoped."

"Where are you now?"

"At my parents' place. We're going out to dinner in a little bit. Oh, listen, shortly after I got back here, Pedicini called me from Corfu. He wanted to know how things were going with Lariani. I told him Lariani was stalling. And so he told me something that at first seemed strange to me."

"And what was that?"

"He suggested I tell Lariani that I was particularly interested in something by Paolo Antonio Barbieri."

"And who's that?"

"Guercino's brother. And a specialist in still lifes."

"And why did that seem strange to you?"

"Because in my opinion it severely narrowed the range of Lariani's search."

"You mean it made things more difficult."

"Or maybe simpler."

"Why?"

"Because naturally I called Lariani immediately and told him that if he had to consult any third parties in his search, he should focus on Barbieri, and he started laughing and said that he'd expected that I would end up asking for him."

"What does that mean?"

"I don't know. But that's enough talking about my business. Can I make a confession to you?"

"Of course."

"I'm starving!"

"Didn't you just say you're going out to dinner soon?"

She laughed.

"Salvo, are you serious or just pretending? I'm starving for you! What about you?"

Though he was alone, Montalbano blushed.

"Naturally," was all he managed to say.

Marian laughed again.

"Good God, sometimes you are so awkward . . . it's adorable. Come on, Inspector, buck up and tell me you want me."

Montalbano closed his eyes, took as deep a breath as possible, and dived in.

"I . . . wa . . . wa . . ." he began.

He froze. Of course he wanted her, he just couldn't bring himself to say it. The words inside him would head towards his mouth enthusiastically, but his lips wouldn't move. They were unable to say them.

"Come on, a little effort. You're almost there," said Marian. "You're better off starting all over."

"I . . ."

Nothing doing. This time the culprit was his throat, which was drier than the Sahara.

"They're calling me to dinner," said Marian. "At this rate it'll take an hour to make you say it. So you're safe for now. I'll call you back before I go to bed, to wish you good night."

He set down the receiver, went out on the veranda, and the telephone rang.

Naturally it was Livia.

"Could you wait just a second?"

He went and drank a glass of water.

"Okay, here I am."

"I tried earlier but it was busy. Who were you talking to?"

"Fazio."

The lie had come to him spontaneously, quite naturally. To the point that Livia swallowed it without hesitation.

By the time he hung up, he figured the number of lies he'd told came to at least ten.

Could he go on this way? No, he couldn't. With every lie he told he felt physically sullied, to the point that he now needed absolutely to go and take a shower.

What a fine example of a man he was!

On the one hand, for all of Marian's effort to wrench it out of him, he'd been utterly unable to tell her even that he wanted her, though he felt that he loved her; and on the other hand he lacked the courage to speak clearly and honestly to Livia, to tell her that he no longer felt that he loved her.

After his shower he felt better and sat down to eat. He scarfed down half of everything and then cleared the table.

He wanted to go to bed early, since he had to get up at six so he could be at the crossroads for Aragona at seven-thirty.

He took the phone and plugged it into the jack next to the nightstand in the bedroom.

Going over to the bookcase, he grabbed the first book that came to hand without even looking. When he lay down he discovered that it was

Stendhal's *On Love*. He laughed and opened it at random.

The first few times I felt love, that strangeness I recognized inside me, it made me think that it wasn't love. I understand the cowardice . . .

He went on reading for a few hours, until his eyes began to flutter. The telephone rang.

"Good night, Inspector."

"Me too," he said clumsily.

Marian started laughing.

"Come on, are you retarded or something? That's the response you should have given me when I asked you if you wanted me too! So this 'me too,' which you uttered through clenched teeth—does it apply to the previous question or does it mean 'I, too, wish you good night'?"

"The second thing," replied Montalbano, feeling at once ridiculous and cowardly.

The right words just wouldn't come to him.

As he was about to leave the house, he was seized by doubt. What if the two Tunisians had seen him on television and recognized him as Inspector Montalbano? It was highly unlikely, but still possible. How was he going to change his appearance in five minutes without having anything in the house that might serve such a purpose?

He made do with a pair of sunglasses that covered half his face, a ridiculous scarecrow hat that came down to his eyes, and an enormous red bandana that he wrapped around his neck in such a way that it came up to his nose. Then he put his fate in God's hands.

He found Intelisano at the crossroads, on time and waiting for him. The farmer looked a little surprised to see him in his getup, but asked no questions.

At a certain point, Intelisano's car stopped in the middle of a dirt road that was nevertheless fairly passable. Montalbano, who was following behind, did the same.

"From here we have to go on foot. Lock your car."

To the left was a path for carts. They took it.

"My property starts here."

They walked for about twenty minutes through freshly plowed land. The scent entered Montalbano's nostrils. The earth smelled as good as the sea.

Then they passed near a stable made of masonry with animals inside. There was a rather large shed made of corrugated metal beside it. The upper part of it was a sort of hayloft.

For a brief moment, as Montalbano was looking, a bright beam of light flashed from the loft and shone straight in his eyes. Despite the sunglasses, he instinctively shut his eyes and when he reopened them the light was gone. He had to take the glasses off and wipe his eyes, which were watering. Maybe it was just a piece of glass that had reflected a ray of sunlight.

9

"That shed is really convenient," Intelisano explained, "because there's a hayloft up top and the ground floor can be used as a garage and for storing equipment, grains, and seeds . . . The farmhands also use it for shelter at lunchtime if the sun's too hot or if it's raining."

"Do they have the keys?"

"Of course."

"And do they also sleep there at night?"

"No, I think I already mentioned to you that they sleep in Montelusa."

After another ten minutes of walking they reached the spot where the Tunisians were working.

Montalbano was able to confirm that, from where they stood, one could not see the other half of the property, the barren part with the ramshackle house, because of a low hill that blocked the view.

But surely the two Tunisians had climbed the hill to work the land up there and thus knew of the existence of the abandoned house.

The two men stopped working. The one on the tractor got down. They doffed their caps. Intelisano introduced them.

"This is Alkaf and this is Mohammet."

"Pleased to meet you," said Montalbano, holding out his hand, which the two men shook.

"They're from Tunisia," Intelisano continued, "and have been workin' here for two years. This is Engineer Carlo La Porta, who's thinkin' of buying this land."

"You sell?" Mohammet asked Intelisano with a look of displeasure.

"Three large properties are pretty hard to keep up with," said Intelisano.

Alkaf smiled at Montalbano.

"You make good buy."

"Even better if you keep us working for you," said Mohammet.

They were both about fifty, but wore their age well. They were slender with intelligent, attentive eyes. Though dressed like paupers, they had an air of distinction about them.

"In Tunisia, did you work for others or did you have some land of your own?" Montalbano asked them.

"Yes, land our own," they said in unison.

"But only a little," Alkaf clarified.

"Did you use tractors?"

"No," said Mohammet, "no money for tractor. Hand-plow and hoe. I learn drive tractor here."

"Shall we continue our visit?" Intelisano asked.

Montalbano nodded yes and took his leave of the two men, shaking their hands again.

Once they were out of sight, Intelisano asked the inspector when he intended to come back to talk to the two men alone.

"I'll be back here by five at the latest. But almost certainly before that."

"Don't forget that when the sun sets they finish workin' and head back to Montelusa."

"Okay."

"What's your impression?"

"They seem sharp, intelligent."

"They are. And great workers."

"So you would tend to rule out that—"

"Inspector, in normal circumstances, they would be two honorable men, but in their current circumstances . . ."

Montalbano felt the same way. They got back to the place where they'd left their cars.

"I'm going to Montelusa, I have some stuff to do there," said Intelisano. "I'll be back here around one or maybe earlier, but I'll make myself scarce for you by three o'clock."

As he was heading back to Vigàta, the inspector felt certain that Alkaf's and Mohammet's hands were not the hands of peasants accustomed to working the land from morning to evening.

When he shook their hands the first time he'd found them relatively smooth, with none of the calluses they should have had.

He'd wanted confirmation the second time. And he got it.

"Good morning, Chief!" said Catarella as soon as the inspector came in.

Montalbano stopped dead in his tracks.

What? He was wearing sunglasses, a ridiculous hat and a giant bandana that made him look like a walking scarecrow, and Catarella recognized him at once, just like that?

"How did you know it was me?"

"Wasn' I asposta know it was you?"

"No. I'm in disguise."

Catarella looked troubled.

"I'm sorry, I din't realize you was diskized. I beckon yer partin, Chief. Bu', if you like, you c'n go back out an' come back in, an' I'll preten' I don'—"

"Never mind. Tell me instead what made you recognize me."

"Well, foist of all, by yer mustashes an' mole. An' seccunly, by yer walk."

"Why, how do I walk?"

"Ya walk the way ya walk, Chief."

In short, he was better off not disguising himself.

"Get me Fazio."

Once in his office he immediately took off his hat, sunglasses, and bandana and shoved them into a drawer of the filing cabinet. He didn't want to do a repeat with Fazio.

"Good morning, Chief. How'd it go with the

Tunisian peasants?" Fazio asked as he came in.

"They may be Tunisian, but they certainly aren't peasants."

"Why not?"

He told him about their hands. Fazio remained pensive.

"But Intelisano says they know how to work the land," he said.

"It's possible that back home they were small landowners, and so they know how it's done. At any rate, I'm going back there this afternoon. I'll have to be very careful about what I say. They're the type that can even read your mind. So what've you got to tell me?"

"Chief, around town they're saying that last night Loredana di Marta was checked into a clinic in Montelusa."

"What happened to her?"

"There are rumors, with nothing confirmed, that she's got a few contusions on her head and some broken ribs."

"Does anyone know how this happened?"

"Well, nobody knows for certain, but some say that it's from the beating her husband gave her over the armed robbery, and others say that she fell down the stairs."

"If you ask me, Signor di Marta must have reached the conclusion that Loredana knew the robber and tried to find out his name by raising a hand and maybe even a foot."

"I agree."

"Now we have to try and find out whether Loredana told him the name or not. Don't you think it's time we had a little look at Carmelo Savastano?"

"Already taken care of."

Montalbano felt irked, as always happened whenever Fazio uttered those four words. On top of everything else, when did the guy find the time to take care of what he said he'd taken care of? The inspector crushed one foot with the other under his desk to calm himself down.

"So fill me in."

"Savastano continues to live the same debauched life as before. Nobody knows where he gets the money to live as well as he does. Yesterday evening he got into a row at the fish market and beat someone up. The carabinieri had him spend the night in a holding cell. By this time he's probably already been released, or will be very soon."

"I think you'd better have somebody keep an eye on him."

"Yes, sir. I wanted to mention something that you ordered me to do. I did it, but you never asked me about it again and I forgot to—"

"What was it?"

"You wanted me to find out how long it might have taken Loredana to get from Via Palermo to Vicolo Crispi."

"You're right. Did you do the test?"

"Yes. Twice. You can't do it in less than half an hour, thirty-five minutes."

He went to eat at Enzo's, taking it slowly. He had time to kill. By the time he came back out, it was almost three.

He decided there was no need to take his customary stroll along the jetty, since he'd be able to digest while walking through the countryside later.

But first he had to drop in at the station to retrieve his sunglasses, straw hat, and bandana.

As soon as he walked in, Catarella assailed him.

"Ah, Chief! Good ting you're 'ere."

"Why?"

"Cuz you best call Signor Intelligiano emoigently an' straightaways-like, cuz he rung 'ere awreddy twice! An' 'e avized 'at ya shoun't go where yer asposta go before 'e called yiz back, 'e bein' 'im, the same Signor Intelligiano."

So what had happened? Montalbano dashed into his office.

"Signor Intelisano, what's going on?"

"Somethin' incredible, Mr. Inspector!"

"What?"

"Somethin' otherworldly!"

"Speak!"

"Somethin'—"

"Are you going to tell me or not?" Montalbano cut him off impatiently, raising his voice.

"Like I tol' you, I went to Montelusa an' was back in Spiritu Santo by twelve-thirty. An' I noticed immediately that the tractor was sittin' in the middle of the field with the motor runnin', but there was no sign of the two Tunisians anywhere."

"Where were they?"

Intelisano didn't even hear him.

"So I went over to the shed. Which was locked, but the keys was just layin' on the ground right in front of the door. So I opened up and went inside. The Tunisians couldna gone too far, 'cause their backpacks was still there with all their other stuff."

"So what did you do?"

"I waited half an hour. Those keys tossed on the ground outside the shed made me think they might come back at any moment. Then, seein' that they wasn't comin' back, I got in my car an' drove to Montelusa. I knew where they lived; they rent a little room in the Rabato. They weren't there. An' the other Tunisians livin' next door tol' me they came back aroun' eleven, grabbed all their stuff in a hurry, an' ran out."

"Where are you now?"

"In Spiritu Santo."

"Please wait for me there. I'm on my way."

Half an hour later he was with Intelisano. Who was sitting out in front of the open shed looking disconsolate.

134

"I can't explain it."

"Then I'll explain it for you. The two Tunisians recognized me, and since they've got something to hide, they ran away."

"So you're saying they had something to do with those weapons?"

"They had a lot to do with those weapons. Their escape proves it."

"But how could they have recognized you?"

"They must have seen me on TV."

Intelisano grimaced.

"'Scuse me for askin', but when was the last time you was on TV?"

Montalbano did some quick calculation in his head.

"About ten months ago."

"And you think that someone that doesn't know you and sees you for a few minutes ten months later's gonna still remember what you look like? Not even if they held a flashlight up to your face . . ."

Flashlight! The flash of light! It hadn't been a reflection off a sheet of metal, but probably . . .

"How does one get up to the hayloft?"

"Behind the shed there's a little iron ladder on the outside, but I never go up there 'cause I'm ascared o' heights."

Montalbano raced behind the shed, followed by Intelisano. The ladder was almost vertical, and dangerous, but the inspector paid no mind, climbing up as nimbly as a fireman, as Intelisano stayed behind on the ground, watching.

The hayloft was practically empty, except for ten or so bales of hay stacked at the back in front of the large window above the shed's main entrance.

Montalbano noticed, however, that the bales had been moved in such a way that a sort of passage was created between them. One could enter it and, from that vantage, see what was going on around the shed.

He went in. The view from up there stretched as far as the spot where he'd left his car and beyond. On top of this, since there was a dip about three-quarters of the way up the small hill dividing the two sections of the property, you could even see the ramshackle house that had served as a temporary arms depot. It was a perfect observation point.

Therefore, when he'd come by that morning with Intelisano, someone had been watching him from the hayloft. Probably with a pair of binoculars, which had then produced the beam of light that had struck him in the eyes.

And it was that person, not the two Tunisians, who'd recognized him. But it explained their hasty escape.

He came back out of the passage between the bales and looked around. In the part of the loft nearest the ladder, someone had arranged enough of a cushion of hay to sleep on.

Beside it was an empty bottle of mineral water. And a folded-up newspaper. Using two pieces of wood, and taking care not to touch it with his fingers, he managed to read the date. It was from that same day. Apparently the Tunisians had bought it early that morning and brought it to the man hiding in the hayloft.

Then he noticed a small plastic bag and opened it with a piece of wood. Inside were the bits of a hard-boiled eggshell, a still-fresh piece of bread, and another bottle of mineral water, half full. Along with the newspaper, they'd also brought him breakfast.

There was nothing else to see. He went back out and down the ladder.

"Did you find anything?" asked Intelisano.

"Yes. The two farmhands were hiding someone in the hayloft. I guess they figured that since you suffer from vertigo, you'd never go up there. He must have been the one who recognized me."

"So what are we going to do now?"

"Close everything up now and come with me to Montelusa."

"What for?"

"To talk to the counterterrorism unit."

Montalbano went into Spòsito's office alone, making Intelisano wait outside.

"Dear Inspector, to what do I owe the pleasure?"

"I'm here to confess to a fuckup on my part."

137

"On your part?" Sposìto asked in surprise.

When Montalbano had finished explaining, Sposìto asked:

"But did the commissioner know you were conducting this parallel investigation?"

"No."

"I get it. Well, for my part, I won't tell him anything."

"Thanks."

"But, look, we don't know for certain that they left because they recognized you."

"We don't?"

"No. What time was it when you and Intelisano left Spiritu Santo?"

"It was probably around nine-thirty, quarter to ten."

"It tallies."

"With what?"

"As I said, we're combing the countryside for those weapons, because I'm convinced they weren't taken very far. This morning at nine, the team working under Peritore, my second-in-command, went back to search the house where the arms had been kept. Then they moved their search towards the hill, looked inside a cave where they found nothing, and looked around a tractor that was stopped farther away, but didn't find anything or anybody. Peritore told me there was also a shed made of sheet metal and a stable. Since they found the keys to the shed outside on the ground, they opened it, looked inside, and found nothing of importance. There wasn't anything inside the stable either. And so they headed for the adjacent property."

"And they didn't look in the hayloft?"

"No. As you see, we're guilty of our own little fuckup."

"So you think the three ran away not because they'd recognized me but because the man in the hayloft saw your men heading for the shed?"

"It's plausible."

"Of course it is. But there's one thing that isn't."

"Oh, yeah? What?"

"That it never occurred to Peritore to send someone to search the hayloft."

Sposito threw up his hands.

"What can I say? It happened."

No, there was something that didn't add up.

"Can I ask you a question?"

"You can ask, but I don't know if I can answer it."

"What kind of net did they tell you to use for your fishing expedition? One with big meshes or little meshes?"

"No comment. At any rate, I'll give Peritore a ring and tell him to go back to the shed and check out the hayloft. There must be fingerprints on the bottle and the newspaper. Happy? While we're on the subject, you didn't touch anything, did you?"

"No. I don't think I did any damage."

Montalbano stood up.

"I brought Signor Intelisano here with me. He owns the property in question. If you'd like to question him about the two Tunisians . . ."

"I certainly do, thanks."

Back in his office, the inspector held a meeting with Fazio and Augello and told them the whole story. And he also mentioned Sposìto's beating around the bush when they discussed it.

"I think I know why he acted that way," said Augello.

"Tell me."

"He's head of Counterterrorism, right? So it's his job to find terrorist cells and discover in time whether some cell is planning an attack against us. Right?"

"Right."

"But what if the people aren't terrorists? What if it involves people who have no intention of doing us any harm and the weapons are supposed to be sent on to their native country to fight the government?"

"Whether they're terrorists or patriots, clandestine arms traffic is still a crime," said Fazio.

"Agreed. But Sposìto doesn't know whether they're terrorists or foreign patriots. You must admit the problem is rather complicated. And so he's handling this with kid gloves."

"You may be right," said Montalbano. "And if

that's the way it is, I'm convinced that Sposìto is hoping soon to raise the issue of conflicting jurisdictions. If they're not terrorists, then it's a case for the Secret Services. Whatever the case, he tried to rid me of the idea that the escape of the Tunisians and the mystery man was my fault. He said it was his team's fault."

"So why would he do that?"

"To get me to drop our investigation, which I had to admit was unauthorized, among other things."

"But we still don't—" Augello cut in.

"Mimì, just think for a second. Sposìto's attitude with me means three things. The first is that he's convinced I was indeed recognized by the man in the hayloft. The second—which stems directly from the first—is that this man is someone who knows me not just in passing but quite well, if he figured out who I was from my mustache, mole, and walk. The third is that the man in the hayloft may not be a foreigner but from Vigàta or some-where nearby. In short, Sposìto was trying to keep me from formulating this argument, which would have made me more curious. At any rate, curious or not, now that the Tunisians have disappeared, we have no more cards to play. So let's talk about something else. Mimì, what have you got to tell me? Have you made contact with Valeria Bonifacio?"

Augello smiled.

10

"Of course I made contact. Boy, did I ever!"

"Don't tell me . . ." Montalbano said in amazement.

"No, we didn't get that far. Don Juan himself couldn't have. But I have to tell you the whole story from the start, because it's interesting. This morning—it must have been around nine—I went to stake out Bonifacio's house in my car, ready to wait a long time. She came out like a bat out of hell at ten, got in her car, and headed for Montelusa. I followed her, naturally. At the Clinica Santa Teresa, she turned onto the driveway and parked in the lot. I did the same as she was entering the clinic. By the time I got to the information desk, she was gone. And so I identified myself, and they told me that La Bonifacio had asked what room Signora Loredana di Marta was in. I didn't know she'd been hospitalized. But I didn't want to waste any time so I didn't ask any questions. I took the elevator to the third floor, which was where I'd been told Loredana's room was. As soon as I was in the hallway I heard some angry shouting. There was a man of about fifty, certainly di Marta, saying: 'Forget about my wife! Don't even think about her! I forbid you to see her! This is all your fault!' To which La Bonifacio retorted: 'Get out of here, *cornuto*!' At which point di Marta grabbed her by the shoulders and pushed her up against the wall. Luckily two nurses intervened. Di Marta went into his wife's room, Valeria headed for the elevators. I managed to get back there before she did. And so we found ourselves inside the elevator together. Since she was crying, I asked her if someone she was close to was very ill. To make a long story short, I took her to the hospital bar. But she didn't want to go in; she wanted to leave. So I persuaded her to come and sit at some other bar nearby that had tables outside. We were there for almost two hours."

"Well done, Mimì. But tell me something: How did you introduce yourself?"

"As Diego Croma, attorney-at-law. I figured it was best to use the same name by which Loredana knows me."

"Did she pour her heart out to you?"

"Not really. She said she was crying in anger, not sorrow, because her best friend's husband had prevented her from seeing her. When I asked why, she said that the husband was jealous of their friendship. And that it was he who had put his wife in the hospital with the beating he'd given her."

"Did she say why he did it?"

"He was jealous, again. But of another man."

"So it took you two hours to get this brilliant result?"

"No, the real upshot was that tomorrow, at four p.m., I'm going to her house. She wants some legal advice from me. And so I started telling her about a court case I was involved in, something I made up on the spot."

"What kind of case?"

"A complicated criminal case in which I come off as an unscrupulous lawyer."

"Why'd you do that?"

"Because I had the impression that La Bonifacio wasn't looking for an honest lawyer."

He'd just got home and was opening the French doors to the veranda when Marian rang.

"Hello, my dear Inspector. How are you?"

"Well, and you?"

"Today was a boring day. Lethally boring."

"Why?"

"I spent the whole day waiting for Lariani's phone call."

"And did he call you in the end?"

"Yes, he finally deigned to call at seven. He told me he found what I was looking for."

"That doesn't seem like such bad news."

"Wait before you say anything. He added that the picture was not in Milan and that I wouldn't be able to see it for another three days. He made me an offer."

"What kind of offer?"

"That while waiting I should come to Switzerland

144

and stay with him at a chalet of his to pass the time. In the end I was convinced."

Montalbano felt his blood run cold.

"You accepted?"

"No, silly. I was convinced that that was a good way to make the time go by."

"I don't understand."

"I'll explain. Tomorrow I'm getting on a plane to Palermo to come back and spend two days with you in Vigàta. And then I'll go back to Milan. What do you think?"

Hearing these words, he felt torn. On the one hand, he would have liked to start jumping for joy; on the other, he felt quite uneasy.

"So, are you going to answer?"

"Look, Livia, normally I would be overjoyed, as you can imagine. But the fact is that at the moment I'm extremely busy. I would only be able to see you in the evening, and there's no guarantee that . . ."

He had the impression that the call had been cut off.

"Hello? Hello?" he started yelling.

Whenever his phone connection was cut off he felt as if some limb had been suddenly amputated.

"I'm still here and my name hasn't changed," said Marian in a voice that sounded as if it were coming from a polar ice floe.

He didn't understand a word she said.

"What that's supposed to mean, that your name hasn't changed?"

"You called me Livia!"

"I did?!"

"Yes, you did!"

He felt annihilated.

"I'm sorry" was all he managed to say.

"And you think that's enough to make up, saying you're sorry?"

He didn't know how to answer.

"Okay, don't worry, I won't come down," said Marian.

"I didn't tell you not to come, I was just trying to explain that—"

"Okay, okay, end of subject. I'll be out late tonight, I'm going to dinner with a girlfriend. I'll call you tomorrow. Good night, Inspector."

Good night, Inspector. Curt, dry. With no "my dear."

His appetite was gone. He went and sat down on the veranda with a bottle of whisky and a pack of cigarettes at his side.

But as soon as he sat down he had to get back up because the phone was ringing. It must be Livia.

Remember that name well, Montalbà: Livia. Don't fuck up again. Once is more than enough.

"Hello?"

"Excuse me for a minute ago. I acted foolishly."

"I . . ."

"No, don't say anything, because when you

146

speak, you only get yourself into trouble. I just wanted to wish you good night again. Good night, my dear Inspector. Till tomorrow."

He hung up, took one step, and the phone rang again.

"Hello?"

"How is it that the phone is busy every evening?"

"And why do you call me only when the phone is busy?"

"What kind of argument is that?"

"I'm sorry, I'm tired. I have two investigations ongoing, and—"

"I understand. Well, owing to a number of circumstances that would take too long to explain, I suddenly have three free days. What do you say I come down to be with you?"

He balked. He hadn't expected this. How was it that all these women suddenly had all this free time?

"It might be a good opportunity to talk things over calmly," Livia continued.

"To talk what over?"

"Us."

"Us? Do you have something to say about it?"

"No, I don't, but I can sense, in my bones, that you have something to tell me."

"Listen, Livia, I should warn you that at the moment I'm extremely busy during the day. I don't have a free moment. We would only be able to talk in the evening. But I don't think I would be in the right condition to—"

"To tell me you don't love me anymore?"

"No, of course not, what are you saying? I would be tired, agitated . . ."

"I get the drift. No need to waste any more breath."

"What do you mean?"

"I mean I'm not coming, since you don't want me."

"Jesus Christ, Livia, I didn't say I didn't want you. I was merely informing you, in all sincerity, that I wouldn't be able—"

"Or willing . . ."

And so began another spat. It lasted fifteen minutes, and by the end of it Montalbano was drenched in sweat.

On the other hand, perhaps in reaction, he suddenly felt hungry as a wolf.

In the refrigerator he found a platter of seafood risotto; in the oven, fried calamari rings and shrimp that he had only to heat up.

He lit the oven and set the table on the veranda.

While eating he kept thoughts of Livia as well as Marian at a safe distance; otherwise his appetite would quickly vanish.

He concentrated instead on Sposìto's attempt to persuade him that the two Tunisians had not fled because the man in the hayloft had recognized him.

Sposito must have had a reason for this.

Was it possible he already had some idea of who this man might be?

And was he perhaps afraid that Montalbano, if he got wind of this idea, might react in the wrong way? The inspector thought long and hard about this, but couldn't come up with an answer.

And in the end he was no longer able to keep his thoughts about his situation at bay.

One thing was certain: that Livia had provided him with the perfect opportunity to talk face-to-face, and he had recoiled. If Marian were to find out that he'd refused to clear things up with Livia, she would surely have called him a coward.

But why was he suddenly so uncertain?

Hadn't he had other love affairs in recent years? Never had he felt so unable to make up his mind. But, if he really thought about it, even this wasn't exactly true. He hadn't mentioned any of those prior affairs to Livia, and that was that.

So why, then, did he feel that he couldn't do the same with Marian?

Wasn't it better perhaps, before talking with Livia, to have a serious talk with himself, poissonally in poisson?

As he reached out to grab the bottle of whisky and pour himself a splash, his elbow struck the ashtray, but he managed to catch it in the air before it fell on the floor and smashed to pieces, being made of glass. It was an ashtray that Livia had bought him and . . .

At that moment he realized he would never be able to reason freely with himself in that house, where the many years of life spent together with Livia were present in every nook and cranny.

In the bathroom hung her bathrobe, in the nightstand were her slippers, in the armoire two drawers were full of her underwear and blouses. Half the armoire, in fact, was filled with her clothes . . .

The glass he was drinking from was bought by her, as were the dishes and cutlery . . .

And the new sofa, the curtains, the sheets, the clothes-stand, the doormat in the entranceway . . .

The house oozed Livia. There was no way he could ever come to a decision freely in that house.

He absolutely had to take at least a twenty-four-hour leave and go far away from Marinella.

But it wasn't something he could do right away. He couldn't just drop the investigations he had under way.

He went to bed.

Before falling asleep he remembered a historical figure he'd studied in school, a Roman consul or something similar, Quintus Fabius Maximus, who'd been nicknamed *Cunctator*, which meant "the procrastinator."

He'd already outscored the old Roman.

• • •

The telephone woke him at seven o'clock the next morning.

"Chief, beckin' yer partin an' all, seein' as how iss rilly oily inna mornin' an' all, but Fazio tol' me as how aspite o' the oiliness o' the hour, I's asposta call yiz an' tell yiz to call 'im an' get ready."

"Get ready for what?"

"Get ready meanin' washin' up an' gettin' dressed."

"Why?"

"Cuz Gallo's gonna come an' pick yiz up in so much as they gotta call sayin' as how there's a car all boint up wit' a cataferous copse isside."

Half an hour later, he was ready. The doorbell rang as he was downing his last cup of coffee.

"Why'd they send you? All they had to do was give me the address and I would have come in my own car."

"You never woulda found it, Chief. It's in a godforsaken place called Casa di Dio."

"And where's that?"

"In the Casuzza district."

He felt a little worried. Could the dream be coming true?

When they got there, he saw that the landscape was exactly like the one he'd dreamt, except that in the place of the coffin there was a burnt-up car.

The peasant was different—or, more precisely,

151

he wasn't a peasant at all but a well-dressed thirty-year-old with an alert look about him. He was standing next to a motor scooter. In Catarella's place there was Fazio.

The air stank of a mixture of burnt metal, plastic, and human flesh.

"Don't get too close; it's still very hot," Fazio warned the inspector.

A body was visible in the passenger's seat. It was all black and looked like a large piece of charred wood.

"Have you informed the traveling circus?" the inspector asked Fazio.

"Already taken care of."

This time the reply didn't bother him. He turned to the young man.

"Was it you who called us?"

"Yessir."

"What is your name?"

"Salvatore Ingrassia."

"How was it that—"

"I live in that house right over there."

He pointed at it. It was the only one in the area.

"And since I work at the fish market, I always have to pass this way to go into town."

"What time was it when you got home yesterday evening?"

"It was probably around nine, at the latest."

"Do you live alone?"

"No, sir, I live with my girlfriend."

"And the car wasn't there when you passed by?"

"No, it wasn't."

"Did you hear anything unusual during the night—say, some shouts or gunshots . . . ?"

"The house is too far away."

"I can see. But here it must be as silent as the tomb at night, and every little sound . . ."

"Of course, Inspector, you're right. And up until eleven o'clock I can assure you I didn't hear anything."

"And so you went to sleep at eleven?"

The young man blushed.

"You could put it that way."

"What's your girlfriend's name?"

"Stella Urso."

"How long have you been together?"

"Three months."

Apparently the couple was too busy with other matters to hear anything, even the bombing of Monte Cassino.

"When do you think the circus will get here?" he asked Fazio.

"Forensics and Pasquano should be here in about an hour, an hour and a half. But I doubt Prosecutor Tommaseo will ever get this far."

It was well known that a seal or kangaroo could drive a car better than Judge Tommaseo. Who, when at the wheel, never missed a chance to get a piece of a tree or pole.

So what was the inspector going to do to pass

the time? Young Ingrassia must have realized what Montalbano was thinking.

"If you'd like to come to my place for a cup of coffee . . ."

"All right, thank you," said the inspector. "Leave your scooter here, we'll take the squad car."

As they headed off, Montalbano asked Ingrassia: "Have you told your girlfriend what you discovered?"

"Yes, I called her on the cell phone right after calling you. She wanted to come on foot to see, but I told her not to."

"Come back and pick us up the moment somebody arrives," Montalbano said to Gallo when they got to the house.

The house was very clean inside and in perfect order. Stella was a pretty girl with a pleasant manner.

When she returned with the coffee, Montalbano asked her the same question he'd asked Ingrassia.

"Last night, did you hear any shouts or gunshots or . . ."

He was expecting her to say no, but Stella turned pensive instead.

"I did hear something."

"Then why didn't I?" said the young man.

"Because you always fall asleep after . . ."

The girl stopped, blushing.

"Please go on, it's important," the inspector coaxed her.

"At some point I got up and went into the bathroom, and that's when I heard a bang."

"What kind of bang?"

"Like a door slamming in the distance."

"So a sharp, sudden noise."

"Yes."

"Could it have been a gunshot?"

"I don't know, I've never heard one."

"Could you tell me, even roughly speaking, what time it was?"

"I can tell you exactly what time it was because before going into the bathroom I passed through the kitchen to drink a little water and I looked at the clock. It was five past one."

They chatted about young Stella's difficulties finding a job of any kind and the fact that she wouldn't be in a position to get married and have children until she found one.

Then Gallo came and picked them up. The Forensics lab had arrived together with Dr. Pasquano, but there was still no news of Tommaseo.

Luckily the chief of Forensics, with whom the inspector shared a mutual dislike, had sent his second-in-command, Mannarino, in his place. He and Montalbano exchanged greetings. The inspector looked on as the Forensics team, dressed up as if for a moon landing, got to work around the burnt-out car.

"Too early to have found anything, I guess?"

"Actually, we *have* found something," said Mannarino.

"Can you tell me what?"

"Sure. A bullet shell. In the backseat area, on the floor. Excuse me for just a minute."

Mannarino returned to his men.

Fazio had overheard the whole exchange. He and Montalbano exchanged glances but didn't say anything. Montalbano went up to a car with Dr. Pasquano sitting inside, angrily smoking a cigarette. It was always best to stay away when the doctor did this, but Montalbano wasn't worried.

"Good morning, Doctor."

"Good morning, my ass."

They were off to a good start.

"What's wrong? Did you lose at poker last night?"

Pasquano was an inveterate poker player but all too often did not have luck on his side.

"No, it went fine last night. I'm just sick and tired of always waiting around for Tommaseo."

"But Tomasseo would be on time if only he never got lost or crashed into trees. You have to feel sorry for him."

"Why should I? I can feel sorry for you, who are on the threshold of senility, but not for someone who's still young."

"And why would I be on the threshold of senility?"

"Because you're showing the symptoms. Didn't you notice what you just called Tommaseo?"

"No."

"You called him *Tomasseo*. Getting people's names wrong is one of the first signs."

Montalbano got worried. Maybe Pasquano was right. Hadn't he called Marian Livia?

"But no need for alarm. It's usually a long process. You still have plenty of time left to screw up."

11

Considering that after another half hour had passed there was still no sign of Tommaseo, and considering that he had run out of cigarettes, and considering that he didn't know what to do with himself, Montalbano decided it was best to have Gallo drive him back to headquarters.

After all, he was just wasting his time hanging around there. His presence was utterly useless.

He didn't have the courage, however, to say good-bye to Pasquano, who'd come out of his car and was pacing swiftly back and forth, four strides forward, four strides back, like a bear in a cage.

Back at the office, having nothing to do, he started signing document after document. There was no end of it.

Fazio straggled back in just before one o'clock.

"Have anything to tell me?"

"Well, Chief, as you were able to see for yourself, before setting the car on fire they took the license plates off. But Mannarino was able to read the serial number on the chassis. I'm expecting an answer at any moment now. We should be able to find out what car it belonged to and who its last owner was. As long as the car wasn't stolen for the occasion."

"Did they find any other shells?"

"No, just that one. But Mannarino said there were tracks from two different cars."

"Naturally. How else would they get back? On foot? And apparently the jerry cans of gasoline for setting fire to the other car were in that one, and once they emptied them out, they took them away, fingerprints and all. Pasquano didn't say anything?"

"He said it'll be hard to identify the body, given the state of the corpse. At any rate, at a glance he said it looked to him that the man had been killed with a single shot at the base of the skull and had his wrists and ankles bound with metal wire."

"A Mafia hit, in short?"

"It certainly looks like one."

"And you're convinced of it?"

"Bah."

Fazio's cell phone rang.

" 'Scuse me just a second," he said, bringing the cell phone to his ear.

He said, "Hello," and then listened silently.

"Thanks," he said in conclusion.

He looked at the inspector, frowning.

"They told me the name of the car's owner."

"Who is it?"

"Carmelo Savastano."

Montalbano digested this bit of news without any difficulty. It wasn't anything that would complicate matters; on the contrary, it might actually simplify them.

"But what's Savastano got to do with the Mafia?"

"Bah," Fazio repeated.

"But it's not certain he's the corpse."

"No, it's not."

"Does Savastano have any family?"

"Yes, his father's name is Giovanni. But they had a falling out and haven't spoken for years."

"You should go and talk to him immediately. Find out whether his son ever broke his leg or has any other distinguishing features that might help to identify the body."

"I'll go right away."

But he didn't move. He looked doubtful.

"What is it?"

"If it turns out to be Savastano, then there's something I found out that I should tell you."

"Let's hear it."

"You know the young guy from this morning, the one who discovered the burnt-up car?"

"Yes, Salvatore Ingrassia."

"Well, he's the guy who got into a row with Savastano at the fish market, after which the carabinieri hauled him in."

"And does Ingrassia seem to you the type who would do something like that?"

"Nah. But I thought I should tell you."

After eating, he took his customary stroll along the jetty. The crab was not there and hadn't sent a replacement.

The inspector started thinking.

If the body was Savastano's, he would bet the family jewels that Ingrassia had nothing to do with the murder. The young man would never have been so stupid as to kill him and leave his body a few hundred yards away from his house.

Whoever killed Savastano either knew nothing about his quarrel with Ingrassia, in which case it was all a coincidence; or else he knew everything about it and committed the murder near Ingrassia's home to throw the police off the track.

Savastano was not a mafioso, but a small-time hoodlum. So why had a Mafia ritual been enacted?

Here there were two possible answers: Either he'd offended some mafioso or other, or else the ritual was supposed to lead the investigation astray.

If, say, Savastano had been found dead on the ground along any old road, shot in the face or the chest—in other words, without any Mafia theatrics—who would have been immediately suspected?

Di Marta, naturally.

The only person who could have had a plausible motive, if he'd grasped how the business of the holdup and rape had really gone.

At the office he found Fazio waiting for him.

"Savastano's father couldn't tell me anything. They hadn't spoken to each other for a long time.

He's just a poor bastard, an honest man who had the misfortune of having a delinquent son. But I may be on to something just the same."

As if a bloodhound like Fazio wouldn't be on to something.

"And what's that?"

"Looking through our papers, I discovered that some time ago a girl who'd been living with him, named Luigina Castro, reported him for domestic violence."

"But wasn't he with Loredana?"

"Yes, but when they broke up because Loredana became engaged to di Marta, he—"

"Got it. Go on."

"Well, Luigina reported him after they'd been together barely two months, but then she withdrew the charges."

"Have you got her address?"

"I've got everything."

"Go and see her right away."

Fazio got up and went out, and a moment later Augello came in. Montalbano looked at him with a bit of surprise.

"But weren't you supposed to be at La Bonifacio's place at four?"

"She called and postponed things till this evening. She invited me to dinner. The prospects are looking good."

"Have you heard about the burnt-up car?"

"Yes."

"Apparently the car belonged to Carmelo Savastano, Loredana's ex-boyfriend."

"And was that him in the car?"

"We don't know yet."

He paused a moment, then asked Mimì:

"If we were to find out that it really is Savastano, who would be your primary suspect?"

"Di Marta. It's possible that he beat Savastano's name out of her."

"Actually, since we haven't been able to discuss it calmly, I'd like to know how *you* think the whole mugging scene went."

"In my opinion, after her marriage, Loredana and Savastano remained lovers. Apparently that evening, when he found out, maybe from Loredana herself, that her husband had given her sixteen thousand euros to deposit, he made an arrangement with her, saying he needed the money. They met, Loredana gave him the money, and then they had rough sex, to make it look like a rape."

"And where does Valeria Bonifacio come in?"

"She comes in to cover for Loredana—who, in my opinion, did go to her friend's house that evening, but left immediately to go meet Savastano. And now Valeria's worried that if you discover the truth, you'll have proof of her complicity. I'm convinced that's why she needs a dishonest lawyer like yours truly."

In a general sense, the inspector saw things the

same way as Mimì. But there were a few details, by no means minor, about which he had a very different opinion.

Around six, Fazio returned.

"I've got something big, Chief. The girl who broke up with Savastano after reporting him for abuse told me he's missing two toes on his left foot. Apparently an iron coffer fell on them, crushing them to smithereens, and he had to have them cut off."

"Excellent. Well done, Fazio!"

Montalbano didn't waste a single minute and immediately rang Dr. Pasquano, turning on the speakerphone.

"Excuse me for disturbing you, Doctor, but—"

"The disturbance you create is of such magnitude and depth that there can be no excusing it."

"My, how well you can speak when you put your mind to it!"

"Thanks. It's you who have this effect on me. Elegant speech comes instinctively to me as a way to put some distance between us. Naturally you'd like to know something about the charred corpse."

"If you would be so kind."

"You are incapable of imitating my eloquence. Or anything else about me, for that matter. So you might as well not even try. I can only confirm what I told Fazio. A single shot at the base of the

164

skull, ankles and wrists bound with metal wire. A textbook Mafia execution."

"Nothing that might help us identify him?"

"Yes. Two—"

"—amputated toes on the left foot," Montalbano finished his sentence.

Pasquano remained speechless for a moment, then exploded.

"But if you already knew, then why the fuck did you have to bust my balls?"

Montalbano hung up and dialed another number.

"Dr. Tommaseo? Montalbano here. I urgently need to talk to you. Can I come by in half an hour? Yes? Thank you."

"What do you want from Tommaseo?" asked Fazio.

"Authorization to put a tap on Bonifacio's and di Marta's phones. Have we got all their numbers?"

"Yessir. Even the cell phones."

"Gimme all of them, including the addresses, and then go and give Savastano's father the bad news."

He was expecting to have to battle with the prosecutor to get permission for the phone taps, but as soon as Tommaseo heard there were two attractive young women involved, he gave in, hoping he'd have a chance to meet them sooner or later.

His eyes began to glisten, and he licked his lips. He wanted to know the whole story of Loredana's rape, down to the last detail.

Just to have Tommaseo on his side, the inspector invented a few details worthy of a porno flick.

Tommaseo wasn't known to have a woman in his life. Interrogating them was perhaps his way of letting off a little steam.

With Tommaseo's authorization in his pocket, the inspector went to Montelusa Central, to the basement facility from which all telephone intercepts were conducted. It took him a good fifteen minutes to pass through all the checkpoints, and over an hour to set the whole operation in motion without delay.

As he was coming out of the building he suddenly thought of a way to verify that Savastano had no business at all with the Mafia. He walked around for five minutes reviewing and examining every aspect of his plan.

In the end, he convinced himself that it was the right move and, on top of that, the only one he had available.

He got into his car and headed for the studios of the Free Channel, the local television station under the direction of a very good friend of his, Nicolò Zito. It was almost nine o'clock.

"Inspector! What a pleasure to see you!" exclaimed the receptionist. "Do you want Nicolò?"

"Yes."

"At the moment he's finishing his news broadcast. You can go and wait in his office."

Zito came in less than five minutes later. They embraced. Montalbano asked after his family and then said:

"I need something from you."

"I'm at your service."

"Have you already broadcast the news of the charred body found in a burnt-up car?"

"Of course. I went there in person this morning to cover the story, but you weren't around, you'd already left. I had to keep to generalities because no one could tell me anything."

"Would you like an exclusive interview?"

"Are you kidding?!"

"Then let's get right down to it. Could you include it in your next news broadcast?"

"Absolutely."

"But first we have to agree on certain questions."

"Inspector Montalbano, thank you for agreeing to meet with us and answer our questions. What can you tell us about this horrific crime, which has upset so many people?"

"Well, for starters, I can tell you the name of the victim. He was a young man from Vigàta, Carmelo Savastano."

"Did he have any sort of criminal record?"

"Yes, but just things like petty scams, illegal appropriation, threatening a public official . . ."

"How was he killed?"

"He was kidnapped somewhere unknown to us, probably as he was going home, and then taken to the place of his execution in his own car, which was driven by one of the killers. Savastano's wrists and ankles were bound with metal wire and he was sitting in the passenger's seat. He was shot once at the base of the skull, and then the killers set the car on fire."

"So, at a glance, everything would point to Mafia-style execution."

"It certainly would, in my opinion. And I intend in fact to conduct my investigation accordingly."

"But do you really think Savastano was a Mafia punk?"

"Don't take it the wrong way, but I'm not at liberty to answer that question."

"Might he have been killed for having made some sort of mistake, or for not obeying orders?"

"I don't think so."

"Could you explain a little better?"

"I'm just hoping this doesn't turn out to be the first in a series of murders in a war between the families, like the one that caused so much bloodshed in our region a few decades ago. That's why I want to do everything in my power, and by every means possible, to nip this thing in the bud. And I'm ready, if necessary, to request exceptional reinforcements of personnel."

He'd lowered the baited hook into the water. He was positive that a fish or two would bite.

When he got home it was ten-thirty. Too late. Surely Marian had tried to call earlier.

His hunger was so extreme that it didn't allow him time to set the table on the veranda.

He ate standing up in the kitchen the *pasta e fagioli* he found in the refrigerator while waiting for the mullet *all'agrodolce* to warm up in the oven.

When the mullets were hot, he pulled them out, put them on a plate, and took this to the chair in front of the television, where he sat down just in time to watch his interview.

It would be rebroadcast on the midnight edition of the news, as Zito had promised.

Having finished eating, he got up and went out on the veranda.

But less than half an hour later he was back in front of the television. At eleven-thirty there was the nightly news on TeleVigàta, the Free Channel's competitor, and he wanted to see whether they would comment on the interview.

The anchor giving the news made no mention of it.

As he was about to wish the viewing audience a good night, a hand holding a sheet of paper came into the picture.

The newsman read it.

"We have just received notice that there appears to have been an exchange of gunfire in the countryside near Raccadali between the police and three non-Europeans who were able to slip through an encirclement by the forces of order. The police have neither confirmed nor denied this report. The incident appears to have involved three non-Europeans with ties to local organized crime. One of them is reported to have been wounded. We have no more details at this time, but will present any updates we may receive in the meanwhile on our twelve-thirty report, in an hour."

For no good reason, Montalbano thought again of Alkaf, Mohammet, and the third man, the one who'd kept hidden in the hayloft.

Might they be the three non-Europeans who clashed with police? And how, if it was indeed them, had they come to such a pass?

At midnight he watched the Free Channel report, which ran his interview again. As for the firefight, Zito only pointed out that one of the three foreigners had been armed with a machine gun and that it was he who fired first at the police.

The whole thing made sense. Alkaf and Mohammet did not seem like men who would fire a gun like that, but the one in the hayloft might well have been armed and ready to kill.

He went to bed reluctantly, putting the telephone on the bedside table just to be sure.

Why wasn't Marian calling?

He started reading, but was too distracted by the thought of Marian and had to reread a page twice because the first time he hadn't understood a thing. After half an hour of this he couldn't stand it anymore and turned off the light, closed his eyes, and tried to fall asleep.

Why wasn't Marian calling?

And why, despite the fact that he had promised himself to do so, had he never asked her for her cell phone number?

And why had she herself never thought of giving it to him?

And why . . .

And why don't two plus two equal three?

The ringing of the telephone awoke him so unexpectedly and so noisily that he was unable, in the dark, to get ahold of the receiver and made the whole thing fall to the floor.

He turned on the light. It was six a.m.

"Hello?"

"Is this Inspector Montalbano?"

A man's voice, which he didn't recognize. He was tempted to tell him he had the wrong number.

All he wanted to hear was Marian's voice.

Then he realized that it would be a mistake to pretend he wasn't himself.

"Yes, who's this?"

"This is Orazio Guttadauro, the lawyer."

In a flash the inspector's brain was completely lucid.

Guttadauro, a sweet-tongued, courteous man, and as dangerous as a snake, was the lawyer for the local Mafia family, the Cuffaros. He was practically their spokesman.

The fish were biting. Montalbano decided to leave him dangling for a spell. One must never appear too interested.

"I'm sorry, sir, but could you please call me back in about ten minutes?"

"Of course!"

He went into the kitchen, prepared the coffee, went into the bathroom, washed his face, returned to the kitchen, drank a mug of black espresso, and fired up a cigarette.

The telephone rang.

He let it ring. Then picked up the receiver after the tenth ring.

12

"What can I do for you, sir?"

"First of all, I beseech you to accept my apologies for calling you at this hour. Surely I woke you up, snatching you straight out of the arms of Morpheus."

"What makes you so sure I was in the arms of Morpheus?"

The lawyer got worried that Montalbano, perhaps not knowing who Morpheus was, might have misunderstood and taken offense at the insinuation. After a moment of perplexity, he clarified:

"I didn't mean in the least to imply . . . Surely you know that Morpheus was the god of sleep, not a human being in the flesh."

"Exactly, counsel. What makes you think I was asleep?"

"Well, then so much the better. I'm at Punta Raisi airport, about to catch a plane."

"Going anywhere interesting?"

"Rome, for the usual business."

Which consisted of speaking with a few indulgent members of parliament or some big-cheese bureaucrats in charge of public contracts, alternating promises with threats.

"Therefore," the lawyer continued, "if I hadn't

called you now, I wouldn't have been able to try you again until after eight o'clock. And I thought that I might no longer find you at home at that hour. And so . . ."

"You could have called me at the office."

"I don't know whether it would have been advisable to disturb you at police headquarters. You're always so busy . . ."

"All right, then. I'm all ears."

"I wanted to tell you that we had the pleasure of seeing you on television last night. We were a veritable chorus of wonderment. Are you aware how good-looking you are?"

"Thanks," said the inspector. *And fuck you and the Cuffaros,* he added in his mind.

"May God preserve your fine health and intelligence for many long years to come," Guttadauro went on.

"Thanks," Montalbano repeated.

One had to be patient with these kinds of people, who always spoke with contorted pretzel logic, never directly. Sooner or later, however, the lawyer would get to the point.

"Last night," the lawyer resumed, "there was a man with us, an elderly peasant of the Cuffaros whom we invite every so often because he keeps us in good spirits with all the marvelous stories he tells. Ah, the age-old peasant culture, now gone forever! This globalization business is destroying our ancient, healthy roots!"

Montalbano understood the game.

"You're making me curious, counsel. I could use a little mood elevation myself. Why don't you tell me one of these stories?"

"But of course, with pleasure! So, there was once a lion hunter on whom his fellow hunters decided to play a joke. Having seen a native who'd killed an ass and covered it with a lion's skin, they bought the animal and hid it amongst the trees. The hunter saw it and shot it. And he had himself photographed with the lion he thought he'd killed. And everyone became convinced that he'd really killed the lion, whereas not only had he not killed the lion, but the lion itself wasn't even a lion but an ass."

"Cute."

"Didn't I tell you? If you only knew how many of these stories he has!"

"And now, counsel, tell me what you—"

"I'm terribly sorry, Inspector, but they've already started boarding my flight. Take care, and I hope to speak with you again soon."

Montalbano smiled, feeling satisfied. The interview had proved to be a good idea.

It was clear that in speaking of "fellow hunters," Guttadauro was referring not only to the Cuffaros, but also to the Sinagras, the rival Mafia family.

They must have called an urgent meeting for the occasion.

The gist of the argument was that the Mafia had

nothing to do with the case, that Savastano was not a Mafia punk (an ass, the lawyer'd said), that he'd been killed by someone not from the Mafia (a native, Guttadauro had specified), and the killing had been made to look like a Mafia hit, when in fact it wasn't.

The inspector had intuited all this from the start, but in Guttadauro's phone call he now had his confirmation.

The call had surely not been made as a favor to him, but only because the mob had been frightened by his promise of sweeping investigations and wanted to be left in peace.

So it was a native who murdered Savastano. Translation from Guttadauro's code: someone from Vigàta who was not in the Mafia.

He rang Fazio.

"What is it, Chief?"

Montalbano told him about Guttadauro's phone call.

"So how should we proceed?" Fazio asked.

"I want Salvatore di Marta in my office at eleven o'clock."

"Why so late? Do you have something to do before that?"

"No. But you do."

"What do I have to do?"

"I want to know everything there is to know about this di Marta."

"Already taken care of."

One of these days I'm gonna kill him, thought Montalbano.

But he said only:

"Then have him come in at nine-thirty. At nine you and I will meet and discuss what to do."

He stayed home until half past eight, dawdling about the house in the hope that Marian would call.

What on earth could have happened to her? He had no explanation for her silence.

At a certain point he thought of looking in the phone book for the number of the mine where Marian's brother worked and finding some excuse for asking him for Marian's number. But he didn't have the nerve.

He waited a bit longer, but still no word from Marian. And the more the minutes passed, the more he realized how much he needed to hear her voice. And so, with all the waiting, he ended up not getting to the office until nine-twenty-five.

"Does di Marta pay the protection racket?"

"Yessir."

"Who does he pay it to?"

"The land his supermarket sits on is in the area controlled by the Cuffaros."

"And who's their collector?"

"A man named Ninì Gengo."

"Think it's possible di Marta arranged something with him?"

Fazio made a wry face.

"Ninì Gengo is not a killer. He's a bloodsucking louse who will only matter until the Cuffaros decide he doesn't matter anymore."

"But don't you think di Marta might have asked Gengo if he knew someone for the job?"

"It's possible. But in so doing, di Marta would end up putting his fate in too many other people's hands."

"You're right."

"And if, on top of that, Guttadauro phoned you specifically to tell you they had nothing to do with it . . ."

"But can we trust the word of a lawyer who's hand in glove with the Cuffaros?"

Fazio shrugged and the telephone rang.

"Chief, 'ere's 'at man called Martha onna premisses again."

"Send him in."

Di Marta was in such a state of agitation that he couldn't keep still for even a second. He squirmed in his chair and was continuously moving his hands, touching the tip of his nose one minute, the crease in his trousers the next, the knot in his tie the next, profusely sweating all the while.

"I'm in trouble, aren't I?" he asked the inspector.

He'd figured it out by himself. So much the better. That would save a lot of time.

"It's true you're not in the best of situations."

Di Marta's shoulders hunched forward as if an immense weight had just been placed on them. He heaved a sigh so long that Montalbano was afraid his lungs might burst.

"I beg you, please, Signor di Marta, to try and remain as calm as possible. And to answer my questions sincerely. Believe me, being sincere could help you a great deal. I also want you to know that this will be a conversation just between us, a private one, so to speak, and it won't be recorded by my colleague here, Fazio. Is that clear? I have no authorization to make any kind of decision. Otherwise I would have told you to bring your lawyer."

Another long sigh.

"All right."

"Can you tell me please where you were the night before last after ten p.m.?"

"Where do you think? At home."

"And was anyone there with you?"

"No. Loredana is still in the hospital. I think they're going to discharge her tomorrow."

"Tell me what you did from the afternoon onwards."

"I was at the supermarket until closing time, then—"

"Just a minute. When you were at the supermarket, did you receive anyone into your private office?"

179

"Yes. A detergent representative and Signora Molfetta, who comes in weekly to pay an installment of her bill with us."

"Nobody else?"

"Nobody else."

"Go on."

"At closing time, I stayed on alone to do some bookkeeping, and then I went to deposit the day's receipts at the bank in Vicolo Crispi, and after that I went home."

"What time was that, more or less?"

"Nine-thirty."

"You didn't eat dinner?"

"Yes, that morning the cleaning lady made me something to eat later for supper."

"What?"

"I don't understand."

"What did she make for you to eat?"

Di Marta gave him a puzzled look.

"I . . . don't remember."

"Why not?"

"I was thinking of other things."

"And after dinner?"

"I watched TV and then went to bed around midnight."

Therefore he had no one who could testify that he'd stayed home the whole evening and night. And this was a point against him. He didn't have what they call a verifiable alibi.

"Why did you beat your wife?"

The question, fired point-blank, made di Marta lurch in his chair.

But he didn't answer.

Montalbano decided to use his imagination a little.

"We know that Signora Loredana told the doctors she fell down the stairs. Clearly she wanted to avoid having to report you. But the doctors didn't believe her; they claimed her injuries were not consistent with a fall. And so they filed a report themselves. I've got it right here in the drawer. Would you like to see it?"

"No."

The ruse had worked.

"Was it you who beat her up?"

"Yes."

"Why?"

"After I found out here that she'd been raped, when we got home I asked her why she hadn't admitted it. I found her answers unconvincing. So unconvincing that I started to think she knew the attacker and wanted in some way to protect him. After which I lost my head and started hitting her."

"So it was only in anger?"

"Yes."

Montalbano frowned sternly.

"Signor di Marta, I advised you, for your own good, to tell the truth."

"But I am . . ."

"No, you're not. You wanted your wife to tell you the name of the man who robbed and raped her."

Di Marta sat there for a moment in silence. Then, as if he'd made up his mind, he replied decisively.

"Yes."

Montalbano realized that from that moment forward, di Marta would be as cooperative as possible.

"And did she tell you?"

"Yes."

"Now you tell me."

"Carmelo Savastano."

"How did you react?"

"I . . . broke down and cried. Then . . . I realized what I'd done and I took Loredana to the hospital."

"Were you thinking of taking revenge on Savastano?"

"I wanted to kill him. And I would have if somebody hadn't beaten me to it."

"How were you planning to kill him?"

"By shooting him the next time I saw his face. Ever since Loredana told me his name, I've been going around with a gun."

Montalbano and Fazio exchanged a quick glance. Fazio stood up.

"Do you have the gun with you now?"

"Of course."

"Stand up slowly with your hands in the air," the inspector ordered him.

Di Marta was halfway up when Fazio grabbed him and removed the pistol from the back pocket of his trousers. He removed the cartridge clip.

"There's one shot missing," he said.

He raised the barrel to his nose and sniffed.

"Have you fired this recently?" he asked.

"Yes," di Marta admitted. "I kept that gun forever in a drawer in my bedside table, and since I'd never used it, never taken it out of the box, I wanted to test it, to see if it worked."

"When did you test it?" asked Montalbano.

"The other evening, in the parking lot behind the supermarket, after everyone had gone home."

"Try to be more specific. You mean the same evening Savastano was murdered?"

"Yes."

"Do you have a license to carry a weapon?"

"Yes."

"Please sit back down."

The strange thing was that the more they spoke, the less nervous di Marta became.

"Let's go back a little in time. Feel up to it?"

"I can try."

"When you first fell in love with your wife, Loredana, she worked for you at the supermarket as a checkout girl, is that correct?"

"Yes."

"We've learned that at the time she was the

girlfriend of Carmelo Savastano. Did you also know this?"

"Yes. Loredana herself told me, once I succeeded in winning her trust. But they weren't getting along very well anymore."

"Why not?"

"Savastano mistreated her. And she would come into my office in tears and pour her heart out to me. I'll tell you a few episodes. One day he spat into the plate she was eating from and forced her to keep eating. Another time he wanted her to prostitute herself to a guy he owed money to. And when Loredana refused, he took a pair of scissors and cut up her clothes. She'd pretty much made up her mind to leave him, but he would blackmail her."

"How?"

"By threatening to circulate compromising photos of her. And even a little video they filmed in the early days of their relationship."

"I see. And what did you do?"

"I convinced myself that I had to confront Savastano."

"Weren't you afraid that, if you found yourself alone with someone like that . . ."

"Of course I was afraid. But by then, Loredana was everything to me."

"Were you carrying a weapon when you went to confront him?"

"No. It didn't even occur to me."

"What did you say to him?"

"I got straight to the point. I wanted to get the hell out of there as quickly as possible. I asked him how much he wanted for leaving Loredana, and to give me all the photos and everything else. I knew he needed money. He was a regular at the gambling dens and didn't have much luck."

"Where did this meeting take place?"

"He'd suggested his place, but I told him I would only meet him out in the open. We met on the jetty."

"Did he accept your offer?"

"Yes, after shilly-shallying a bit."

"How much was it?"

"Two hundred thousand in cash, a hundred upon his delivery of the material requested, and a hundred on the eve of my marriage to Loredana."

"Why wait until the marriage?"

"So that I could be certain that he wouldn't harass Loredana, who'd gone to stay with her parents during the wait. It would have cost him half the sum agreed upon, so it wasn't in his best interest. Then if, after the wedding, he got it into his head to reappear, I would defend Loredana myself."

"Did he abide by the agreement?"

"Yes."

"Do you still have the material Savastano turned over to you?"

"No, I destroyed it."

"Assuming everything you've just told us is true, what reason do you think Savastano could have had for robbing and raping your wife?"

Montalbano was expecting the answer di Marta gave.

"I think he was put up to it."

"By whom?"

"By Valeria Bonifacio."

"And what motive would Signora Bonifacio have for—"

"Because she hates me. To do me harm. Because she's jealous of Loredana's love for me."

"But do you have any proof at all to support this claim?"

"No."

Montalbano stood up. Di Marta likewise.

"Thank you. I don't need you anymore."

Di Marta seemed doubtful.

"So I can go?"

"Yes."

"And what happens next?"

"I'm going to talk with the public prosecutor. He'll decide on the next step to take."

"What about my gun?"

"It stays here. Anyway, what do you need it for? Savastano's dead now."

Fazio showed di Marta out. When he returned, Montalbano asked:

"So, what do you think?"

"Chief, he's either a clever rogue playing a

186

difficult game, or just some poor bastard who's up to his neck in shit. What do you think?"

"I think exactly the same as you. But in the meantime we should assign ourselves some homework for the vacation. While I go and talk to Tommaseo, you should take di Marta's gun to Forensics. They've still got the bullet that killed Savastano, and we can see if it was shot by this gun. Then you have to try to find something out."

"And what's that?"

"Did you hear the news about a firefight between police and three foreigners?"

"Yes. And I thought the same thing as you, that it might be the three men in Spiritu Santo."

"If I dare to ask Spòsito for a few details, the guy's sure to cuss me out or refuse to answer. If, however, you could talk to a few of your colleagues . . ."

"Got it. I'm on my way."

But he didn't get out in time, because at that moment Mimì Augello walked in.

13

"I didn't come in earlier because Catarella told me di Marta was with you. Not knowing whether I should enter or not, I figured it was best to stay away."

"You were right, Mimì."

"Want to hear how my dinner with La Bonifacio went?"

"If it's not a long story . . ."

"It's rather short, actually."

"Then have a seat and tell us," said Montalbano.

"For the first part of the evening, Valeria played the saint. She acted like she'd just come down from heaven, believe me. Demure, eyes lowered, high-necked blouse, skirt below the knee. She told me the story of her life, starting with elementary school. She told me how unhappy she was as a little girl because her father had a mistress who had a son from him. And so family life was one big quarrel. As she was recalling all this, she wiped her eyes with a handkerchief. She wanted me to believe that her husband had been, and continues to be, the only man in her life. That the months and months he's away weigh heavy on her, yes, since she's a girl with a healthy, indeed remarkable constitution, but her privations are compensated by the great love that holds them together like ivy—her exact words. In short, a crashing bore that continued until eleven o'clock."

"And what happened at eleven o'clock?"

"Well, the television was on, and you, Salvo, appeared on the screen. Upon hearing the news of Savastano's death, she changed completely, turned into a madwoman, screaming that the killer was surely Loredana's husband. I tried to calm her down, but it only made things worse. She had a hysterical fit, broke a dish, tried to head-butt the wall, and so I had to take her by force into the bathroom, wash her face, and put her head under the shower. So she got all wet. She wanted to change clothes but was unable. Her hands were trembling too much and she couldn't stand on her own two feet, so she was leaning against me. I was the one who had to take off her blouse and bra and put some dry clothes on her. And her skirt, too."

"But not her panties?"

"No, those were dry."

"And then?" asked Montalbano and Fazio in unison.

"Sorry, but I have to disappoint your piggish male expectations. She showed me the merchandise, real top-notch stuff, but I realized that it wasn't for sale that evening. She told me she needed to go to bed, and so I kissed her hand like a true gentleman and left. I'm going to see her again this evening, and we're having dinner together."

"And in conclusion?"

"In conclusion, she's a terrific actress. And a bitch on wheels. Cunning and dangerous. She put on a tragic scene with mastery. I'm sure she was intending to say something to me against di Marta, but your TV appearance fell out of the sky and she grabbed it on the fly and ran with it. She's taking things step by step with me. Tonight we'll see how far she goes. Speaking of which, Beba's been grumbling that I'm never at home anymore. Don't be an asshole this time: please tell her I'm on a job. How'd things go with di Marta?"

"Badly, at least for him."

"Meaning?"

"He doesn't have a verifiable alibi for the night of the murder. And he's got the motive. I'm going to talk with Tommaseo now, but the guy's sure to issue a notice of investigation to di Marta. In fact, we'll be lucky if he doesn't have him arrested."

Arriving at the courthouse, he was told that Tommaseo was busy in court and would be tied up until one o'clock.

He'd been stupid not to phone ahead and find out whether the prosecutor could see him.

Since he had the time, he went to Montelusa Central to see how the phone taps were coming along. When he got to the basement he was told that for the case concerning him, he should go to booth 12B.

Inside was a uniformed officer wearing headphones and doing a crossword puzzle. Two people could barely fit in the booth.

"I'm Inspector Montalbano."

"Officer De Nicola," said the other, standing up.

"At ease. At what time did you start the intercepts?"

"Seven o'clock this morning."

They'd been quick about it, he couldn't complain.

"Have any calls been made?"

"Yes. If you'd like to listen . . ."

"Of course."

De Nicola sat him down beside him, gave him another headset, and pushed a button on a sort of computer. The policeman then listened to the recording again with him.

"Hello?" said a woman's voice.

"Hey, Valè, how are you doing?"

"Loredà, my angel, my darling, any news as to when they'll decide to discharge you?"

"Tomorrow for sure. My husband got called in to the police for questioning."

"Think they'll arrest him?"

"I don't know how it'll turn out, but it certainly doesn't look good for him. Listen . . ."

"I want to ask you . . . Everything okay?"

"Are you referring to . . ."

"Yes."

"Don't worry, everything's fine."

"Swear?"

"I swear."

"Valè, I can't take it anymore, I'm going crazy in this place, not being able to—"

"Calm down, please. Don't do anything stupid. Just be patient. You'll have plenty of opportunity to make up for time lost."

"I have to go now. The doctor's coming in."

Then there was another call to Valeria. A man's voice, rather young-sounding.

"Valè, iss me."

"You must be insane!"

"Valè, just lissen to—"

"No. And don't call back unless I tell you to beforehand."

And Valeria hung up.

"Can you tell me where that second call came from?"

"From a cell phone connected to the Montereale network. That's all I can tell you."

"Could I have a copy of that recording?"

"What kind of recorder have you got?"

Too complicated.

"Actually, just get me a sheet of paper and I'll write it all down. They're not long conversations, after all."

"Technically any transcription is supposed to be authorized by the prosecutor," said Officer De Nicola. "But I think I know a solution. Will you grant me permission to take a coffee break?"

"By all means."

"Thanks. Here, use my headset. If you happen to hear a telephone ringing, first press this button, then this one. And you'll find all the paper you need here, in this drawer."

Luckily there were no phone calls. Otherwise God only knows what kind of mayhem he would have unleashed.

He went back to the courthouse, waited awhile, and was finally able to meet with the prosecutor.

"But it's ten past one! It's time for—"

"Sir, this is about that case with the two girls, remember?"

Montalbano had touched his weak spot.

"Of course I remember! Look, I'll invite you to lunch. That way we can talk it over calmly."

Montalbano broke out in a cold sweat. God only knew what sucky sort of restaurant Tommaseo would take him to. The prosecutor was the kind of person capable of dining on wild berries and dog meat.

"All right," said the inspector, resigned.

Instead he ate a decent meal. He had no complaints, even though he was forced to talk while eating, contrary to habit.

When they'd finished, they went back to Tommaseo's office.

"How do you intend to proceed?" asked Montalbano.

"Given this di Marta's hours, I'll send two carabinieri to pick him up at the supermarket at four p.m. That way we can be sure to find him there. The carabinieri will give him time to find his lawyer, and then escort him, with his counsel, to my office."

Montalbano made a rather doubtful face, and Tommaseo noticed.

"Is anything wrong?"

"If you send the carabinieri to the supermarket, someone will inform the press, the TV stations, and . . ."

"So what?"

"As you wish, sir. I simply wanted to warn you that the store will be under siege. Is my presence needed?"

"If you've got other things to do . . ."

"Then, with your permission, I won't be there."

"Oh. Listen, Montalbano, when did you say di Marta's beautiful wife will be discharged?"

"Tomorrow."

"Then I'll nab her tomorrow," said Tommaseo, licking his lips like a cat at the thought of a mouse.

• • •

It was three-thirty when he got back to headquarters. Fazio immediately joined him in his
office.

"I left the pistol with Forensics. They're gonna
call me later with their answer."

"Did you talk to anyone in Counterterrorism?"

"Yes. The team had been on the trail of our
friends from Spiritu Santo for two days."

"So it was them?"

"Yessir."

"And they were the ones who'd turned the
ruined house into an arms depot? Was this
confirmed?"

"Yessir. Apparently they'd been involved in
arms shipments to Tunisia for some time. They
weren't doing it for money, but because they
oppose the current government and are planning
a revolution. Sposìto's orders were to arrest
them but to avoid as much as possible any
gunfire."

"So how did it turn into a shootout?"

"The three men were hiding in a grotto, which
the team had just passed in front of without
noticing anything, when they heard a burst of
machine-gun fire right behind them. They blindly
fired back, but the three managed to escape."

"Are you telling me they only heard the
machine-gun fire?"

"Yes."

"So it's possible it went off accidentally?"

"That's what they thought, too. They also told me that one of the three was definitely wounded. They found quite a lot of blood."

After Fazio left, the inspector started signing papers. He was planning to leave the office early and be back home in Marinella by eight at the latest. He wanted to avoid doing a replay of the previous evening. By now he was convinced that Marian had tried to call but he hadn't been home.

Fazio reappeared around six-thirty.

"It doesn't match."

"What doesn't match?"

"The rifling on the barrel of di Marta's pistol doesn't match the marks on the bullet extracted from Savastano's head. He was shot with a pistol of the same caliber, a seven-sixty-five, just not di Marta's."

This was a point in di Marta's favor.

"Does Tommaseo know this?"

Fazio shrugged.

"Dunno."

A little while later Augello came in to say good-bye.

"Isn't it a little early for dinner?"

"First I have to go home and change."

"You gonna get all spiffed up?"

"Of course. And douse myself in cologne."

"What's it called?"

"The cologne? *Virilité*."

"And are you still up to the promise of this cologne?"

"I can't complain."

He was about to get up and go out when the outside line rang. It was Zito.

"Can I come by in about twenty minutes?"

"What for?"

"Will you grant me an interview?"

"What about?"

"Come on, you mean you don't know?"

"No. What happened?"

"Tommaseo arrested di Marta."

Montalbano cursed, not about the arrest but because of the interview request.

How could he say no to Zito, who had done him so many favors in the past? But that might very well cause him to get home late, and Marian . . .

"All right, but try to get here as soon as you can."

He immediately called the prosecutor.

"Dr. Tommaseo? Montalbano here. I heard that—"

"Yes, the evidence is there, and it's quite damning. If we let him run free, we risk tainting the evidence. And he might even harm his wife again."

"You should know that Forensics checked the

pistol I confiscated from di Marta and they didn't—"

"Yes, I know, they let me know during the interrogation. But that doesn't change the overall picture."

"Let's make this snappy, so I can air it on the nine-thirty news broadcast," said Zito, coming in with a cameraman.

"And if you can manage to be out of here in fifteen minutes I'll kiss you on the forehead."

Five minutes later they were ready.

"Inspector Montalbano, thank you for being so kind as to talk with us. So now we have Carmelo Savastano's killer. My compliments to Prosecutor Tommaseo and yourself. You moved quickly."

"First of all, I'd like to make clear that neither I nor Prosecutor Tommaseo believe that it was di Marta who physically carried out the killing. If anything, he was the instigator."

"Prosecutor Tommaseo told us that revenge was the motive. But he wouldn't say any more than that."

"If Prosecutor Tommaseo limited himself to saying only that, then it's certainly not up to me to add anything."

"But was that the only motive?"

"If that's what the prosecutor said . . ."

"People are whispering that di Marta had Savastano killed out of jealousy."

"I have no comment on that."

"Have you questioned Salvatore di Marta's wife, who is presently in the hospital due to a fall?"

"Yes."

"Can you tell us whether Signora di Marta—"

"No."

"But do you have material evidence against her husband?"

"Not yet, but we have strong circumstantial evidence."

"Is it true that you confiscated a handgun belonging to di Marta?"

"Yes."

"It's been said that your Forensics department, after examining it, has ruled it out as the murder weapon. Can you confirm or deny this?"

"I can confirm it. It was not the murder weapon. Just the same, I would like to point out that we consider di Marta the instigator of the crime, and therefore the fact that his pistol was not the one used in the killing is irrelevant."

"So the investigation to find the material executor of the crime is still ongoing?"

"Of course. But it involves two persons."

"Thank you, Inspector Montalbano."

When Zito and his cameraman left the office, Montalbano looked at his watch. Past eight-thirty. But there was one more thing he had to do, and he thought it was important.

He called Augello on the cell.

"Where are you?"

"In my car. I'm on my way to Valeria's."

"Did you know that Tommaseo had di Marta arrested?"

"Yes. I heard it on the eight o'clock news."

"I wanted to let you know that at nine-thirty there's an interview with me on the Free Channel. I want you to observe how Valeria reacts this time."

"No problem. She always has the TV on."

He dashed to the car and sped home.

As he was opening the door he heard the phone ringing. But he managed to pick up the receiver in time.

"Hello?" he said, out of breath.

"Ciao, Inspector. Been running?"

He heard bells chiming, birds singing, guitars playing, fireworks popping in his head.

A deafening uproar.

"Yeah. I just got in. I want . . . I want everything from you, immediately."

Marian giggled.

"Gladly, but how?"

"No, I'm sorry, what were you thinking? I meant I want you to give me all your telephone numbers."

"Don't you already have them?"

"No, and I keep forgetting every time to . . ."

"Okay. Let me give you my cell phone and my parents' number."

He jotted these down on a piece of paper.

"Why didn't you call me last night?"

"I'll tell you later. It was a stupid idea I had that turned out to be wrong."

"Could you be a little clearer?"

"I was just on my way out. Can I call you around midnight?"

"Of course."

"Until then, Inspector."

He suddenly felt hungrier than a wolf on the Siberian steppes.

With a kind of inner howl, he set out in search of his quarry—that is, whatever it was that Adelina had cooked for him. He yanked the refrigerator open with such force that the door nearly came off in his hand.

Hymns of thanksgiving were the only fitting tribute that could be paid to what he found—two dishes like two Van Gogh suns shining with their own light: risotto with artichokes and peas for the first course, and fresh young tuna in tomato sauce as the second.

As the dishes were warming up, he went and

opened the French door to the veranda. He was surprised to see that it had started raining lightly, in what Sicilians call a peasant-drenching drizzle. But it wasn't at all cold, so he could eat outside.

The mist accentuated the scent of the sea, which he breathed in deeply, filling his lungs.

The sand, too, had a pleasant smell about it.

And the gentle sound of the raindrops on the porch roof was like a distant melody that . . .

What the hell had gotten into him?

How was it that he so suddenly appreciated the same rain that had always put him in a bad mood?

Was it the inevitable change that came with age which made him more understanding?

Or was it much more likely the "Marian effect"?

He decided not to watch his interview, which was about to come on.

He set the table, waited for the rice to get nice and hot, and then brought it outside.

He savored it down to the last pea and grain of rice.

Then he moved on to the tuna, which he gave the same reception as the risotto.

Then he cleared the table, grabbed his cigarettes and an ashtray, and went back out on the veranda.

No whisky this time. He wanted his mind to be lucid.

From his pocket he extracted the sheet of paper with the transcriptions of the intercepted phone calls and started studying them.

14

The first thing that jumped out at him like a black blot on a white sheet was that neither Valeria nor Loredana exchanged so much as a single word on the murder of Carmelo Savastano.

After all, it wasn't as if a lot of time had passed since news of the identification of the body had come out.

Maybe they'd already touched on the subject in some prior phone call before the line had been tapped. But in any case it seemed as if the two girls were glossing over a very important matter. As if they had expressly agreed not to talk about it.

And this was very strange.

Until proven otherwise, Savastano, aside from having spent a long time with Loredana as her boyfriend and master, had also been her mugger and rapist.

The very fact that she was now in the hospital was in a certain sense a consequence of her intimate acquaintance with the murder victim.

How was it that not a single word about him, either of insult or compassion, had ever come out of the girl's mouth? Savastano had suffered a horrific end. You'd think that some sort of heartfelt exclamation—"Poor guy!" or "He deserved it!"—would be forthcoming.

But no.

And how was it that Valeria, who with Mimì made a great show of accusing di Marta, made no mention of the fact that Loredana's husband had been summoned by the police for questioning? Shouldn't she have expressed some hope that they would send him straight to prison?

Too many omissions, too much silence.

And there were some other things that were utterly incomprehensible.

Loredana's questions, when she wanted to know if everything was okay and said she was going crazy having to stay in the hospital, without being able . . .

Without being able to do what?

And then Valeria's reassuring reply, when she said she would have plenty of opportunity to make up for time lost . . .

Make what up? And with whom?

Whatever the case, it was clear that Valeria was the only link between her friend and the thing that Loredana missed so much.

As for the second phone call, it was probably best not even to try. It was impossible to understand anything about it at all.

But the tone of Valeria's voice when he'd heard the recording with his own ears had given him a clue.

Valeria's immediate reaction had been somewhere between astonishment and fear. Or better yet, it contained both astonishment and fear.

She'd said: "You must be insane!" But she'd stopped short, hadn't finished her sentence. She must surely have been about to say "to call me on the phone."

So there must have been a prior agreement between Valeria and the caller, made who-knows-when. That the man must not call for a certain amount of time. And the man had not kept his word.

But given that Valeria was at home alone at the time of the call, as she nearly always was—and therefore no one could overhear her talking to the man—why was she so against talking to him over the phone?

If he was just a lover, she certainly would have had no problem talking to him.

Therefore he was not a lover.

So what was he?

And who was Valeria afraid might overhear her conversation with him?

Certainly not her faraway husband. Nor Loredana in the hospital.

Then who?

Want to bet Valeria thought her phone line might be tapped?

If that was the case, this meant that any contact with that man constituted a potential danger for her.

Mimì's mission was becoming more and more crucial.

• • •

The phone rang at eleven-thirty. It was Livia.

"I'm going to bed. I just wanted to wish you good night."

Her voice sounded like she had a cold.

"Are you okay?"

"No."

"What's wrong? Do you have a fever?"

"I don't think so, I don't know, this has never happened to me before."

"But what are you feeling?"

"Ever since I woke up this morning I've been feeling like I want to cry."

He got worried. It wasn't as if tears came so easily to Livia.

"And I don't even feel like talking. I just want to sleep. I'm going to take a sleeping pill after I hang up. I'm sorry."

"No, *I'm* sorry."

It came straight from his heart. It was all his fault. But then Livia said something he hadn't expected.

"You have nothing to be sorry about. It has nothing to do with you, or with our current situation."

"Then why?"

"I told you. I don't know. I don't understand. I feel a kind of looming emptiness, a loss that can never be filled. My own, personal loss. It's a bit like when I learned that my mother had an incurable illness. Something like that. But I don't want to depress you. Good night."

"Good night," said Montalbano, feeling like a cad.

And he was a cad. But he couldn't help it.

He grabbed the phone, brought it into the bedroom, went to the bathroom, then lay down in bed.

He lay there belly-up, staring at the ceiling, unable to get Livia out of his head.

When, just before midnight, the phone rang, it was like a gust of wind that blew away any thought that didn't have to do with Marian from his mind.

"Hello, Inspector."

"Hello. How's it going with Lariani?"

"What can I say? Today he phoned to tell me that he will almost certainly have two paintings for me the day after tomorrow."

"Let's hope this time it's for real."

"Let's hope, because wasting all these days isn't something I . . ."

"Can you tell me why you didn't call me yesterday?"

Marian giggled.

"Why are you laughing?"

"Because sometimes you assume this inquisitorial, coplike tone of voice."

"Sorry, I didn't mean to, I only wanted—"

"I know. Do you really want to know?"

"Yes."

"Well, I realized that after I talk to you, I have trouble getting you out of my head. It intensifies my thoughts of you. And the more I think of you, the more I'm overwhelmed by the desire to be with you. And since I can't be with you, I become cross and distracted and sometimes can't fall asleep. So I wanted to do an experiment, and I didn't call you. That made it even worse. And so here I am again, talking to you from Milan. I can't stand it any longer, I'm going crazy here, not being able to . . ."

It was like a thunderbolt.

"Holy shit!"

It just came out.

"What is it?" Marian asked in surprise.

"Finish the sentence, finish the sentence!"

"What sentence?"

"The one you were saying, that you couldn't stand it any longer, you were going crazy there, not being able to . . ."

"Have you lost your mind?"

"Please, I beg you, I implore you: not being able to what?"

There was a pause.

When she finally spoke, Marian's voice was icy and mocking.

"To hug you, silly. To kiss you, moron. To make love to you, stupid."

And she hung up.

She'd used almost the exact same words as

Loredana! Wasn't it possible Loredana was in the same position as Marian?

But now he had to repair the damage immediately.

He tried calling Marian on her cell phone. It rang and rang. He called her on her land line. No answer. Maybe she'd unplugged it. The fourth time he tried her cell phone, Marian finally answered.

It took them half an hour and then some to make up.

Then Marian wished him good night with her usual loving voice.

And he was able to sleep soundly.

At the station he found Mimì and Fazio waiting for him.

"I'm here to report," said Augello.

"You look fresh as a rose this morning," said the inspector. "So Valeria didn't wear you out?"

"I'm still not there yet."

"So where are you?"

"I got her to display the merchandise again and let me taste-test the freshness. I declared myself madly in love with her and ready to do anything for her."

"I see. And how did she react to my interview?"

"I'm convinced that it was only after seeing you on TV that she got the idea to let me taste the merchandise. At a certain point, when I was hoping to go from tasting to purchasing, she stopped me and asked me if I was prepared to take a big gamble for her."

"Were those her exact words?"

"Yes. 'To take a big gamble.'"

"And what did you say?"

"That I was ready to give my life for her."

"Was there any background music?"

"Absolutely. From the television."

"Who knows what she has in mind?" Fazio cut in.

"I'm going to find out this afternoon, you can count on that," said Augello. "She's expecting me at four. Apparently it's going to take a while."

The meeting broke up.

"Ahh, Chief! Ahh, Chief Chief!"

Whenever Catarella intoned this litany you could be certain that it had something to do with Hizzoner the C'mishner, as he called him.

"Did the commissioner call?"

"Yessir, 'e did. An' 'e's still onna line!"

Montalbano imagined Commissioner Bonetti-Alderighi as a scruffy crow perched on an electrical line.

"Put him through."

"Montalbano?"

"What can I do for you, Mr. Commissioner?"

"Could you dash over here as quickly as possible?"

"As quickly as it takes me to get there."

He got in his car and drove off. Normally, when the commissioner summoned him, it was to give him a solemn scolding, rightly or wrongly, and therefore Montalbano made a conscious effort to remain calm, whatever his boss might have to say to him.

The commissioner received him at once.

He must not have been feeling well, because his face had the same yellowish cast it had when he rose out of his coffin. He was even polite.

"Dear Montalbano, please sit down. How are you?"

Never before had Bonetti-Alderighi asked him this. Perhaps the end of the world was nigh?

"Not too bad, thanks. And yourself?"

"Not too well, but I'll get over it. I asked you here to find out whether, aside from the Savastano murder, you have any other investigations in progress."

"No, none."

"Now answer me frankly: Could this ongoing investigation be carried on by Inspector Augello?"

"Of course."

"Good. As perhaps you already know, Commissioner Sposito and the rest of the counter-terrorism unit are engaged in a manhunt for three Tunisians involved in illegal arms traffic and hiding out in our province. The area they have to cover is too vast, and Sposito asked me this morning, before going out to join his men in the field, to provide some backup. I think you and a couple of your men would suffice . . . We're only talking about two or three days."

The commissioner had no idea how deeply immersed the inspector was in this affair.

"That's fine with me," said Montalbano.

"Thank you. I just wanted to make sure you were available before discussing it with Sposìto. I'm sure he'll be pleased when I tell him."

The commissioner stood up, shook the inspector's hand, and smiled.

Montalbano felt numb as he left the office, seriously concerned for Mr. C'mishner's state of health.

But while he was there, he might as well go all the way.

He went downstairs to the basement. In booth 12B De Nicola was still doing crossword puzzles.

"Good morning. Any calls?"

"Yes. One from the husband, at eight o'clock, another at eight-thirty from a lady asking for a charitable contribution, and then at nine, Signora Bonifacio called Signora di Marta."

"Let me hear the last one," said the inspector, putting on the headset.

"Loredà, darling, what time are they releasing you?"

"At noon."

"I'll come and pick you up in my car. I can't believe we'll be together again. It doesn't seem real."

"I can't believe it either. Oh, goody! Listen, don't get mad, but did you tell anyone I was getting out?"

"No, I didn't."

"Why not?"

"Because for now it's better this way."

"But I . . ."

"It's better this way, I tell you. And don't make me repeat it a thousand times. Did you hear about your husband?"

"Yes. I have a TV in my room."

"I met someone who might be a big help to us. I'm working him over pretty good."

"Who is it?"

"A lawyer. His name is Diego Croma."

"What did you say his name was?"

"Diego Croma."

"I think I've met him. And why do you think he could be useful to us?"

"I'll tell you when we're together. See you later."

"Should I go and have a coffee?" De Nicola asked, smiling.

Montalbano gave him a confused look.

"You don't need to transcribe this one?"

213

Montalbano remembered and smiled.

"No, thanks."

Not a word of comment from the two women about di Marta's arrest. And Loredana found herself up against a wall when she wanted to get back in touch with someone against Valeria's wishes.

He didn't drop in at the station, but went straight to Enzo's for lunch. Afterwards he took a stroll along the jetty and sat down on the flat rock. The crab scurried into the water the moment it saw him. Apparently it didn't feel like playing. Most likely crabs themselves had their bad days and dark moods.

By now it was clear that the person who had to be placed at the center of the whole investigation into Savastano's death was Valeria Bonifacio. And perhaps letting Mimì handle everything was the wrong approach. It was time to get Fazio involved too.

He returned to the office.

"Ah, Chief! C'mishner Sposato called sayin' if ya call 'im straightaways 'e'll be there."

"Cat, you wouldn't happen to mean Commissioner Sposìto, would you?"

"Why, wha'd I say?"

"All right. Ring 'im and put the call through to me."

"Montalbano?"

"What can I do for you? I spoke with Commissioner Bonetti-Alderighi and am ready—"

"That's why I'm calling. I told the commissioner that's not what I need."

"I don't understand."

"I think the commissioner misunderstood what I said. I told him I needed men."

"And what am I, a horse?"

"I need grunts, Montalbà, not someone like you."

"Ah, I see. You don't want me in your hair."

"Oh, come on! That's the furthest thing—"

"Are you worried I might steal your thunder if they're caught?"

"Oh, fuck off! At any rate, I don't want you. Got that?"

"Got it."

Sposìto seemed to be having second thoughts.

"I'm sorry, Montalbano, but the circumstances—"

"Now you fuck off."

He didn't know Sposìto could be so petty. And what were these circumstances, anyway?

There was something about this that didn't add up.

He'd provoked Sposìto on purpose, but the guy didn't fall for it.

He thought for a second of calling Bonetti-Alderighi and demanding an explanation, but then decided to let it drop.

Maybe it was better this way. He would be

spared the long treks across the countryside in the sun and rain, where he might even be forced to eat lamb stew or blood sausage, stuff he refused to put in his mouth, at the home of some shepherd or other.

He summoned Fazio and had him read the transcriptions of the two intercepted phone conversations. Then he described the exchange he'd overheard that morning.

"What do you think?"

Fazio basically made the same observations he had, and concluded that Bonifacio was up to her neck in this.

"So this is where you come in, Fazio. You've already told me a few things about Valeria Bonifacio, but it's not enough. We have to dig deep into her life. We have to know everything about her, everything."

"It won't be easy, but I can try."

"Get on it right away."

"Oh, there was something I wanted to tell you. Di Marta's supermarket reopens tomorrow."

"Was it closed?"

"Yes."

"So who's going to manage it?"

"Di Marta had his lawyer give his wife power of attorney."

"Does di Marta have other properties as well?"

"The guy's loaded, Chief. He owns ware-houses, homes, land, fishing boats . . ."

$$\bullet \quad \bullet \quad \bullet$$

Augello shuffled back in around seven.

"Got any news for us?"

"Yes. As I said, I went to Valeria's at four. She received me in a state of undress, wearing only a little bathrobe that opened up when she walked, showing her panties and bra."

"In battle gear."

"That's exactly right. But since she's careful only to dole it out in small doses, she didn't take me into the bedroom. We stayed on the sofa doing everything you can possibly do without doing the main thing. She has remarkable control; she was always able to stop me in time."

"But did she tell you anything?"

"Salvo, you've got to believe me, the girl's a master. She mentioned some package she was going to give me but which wasn't for me personally. When I asked her who I was supposed to give it to, she started laughing. But she explained that I wasn't supposed to give it to anyone or even show it to anyone. I was simply supposed to put it somewhere without being seen. If I was discovered, I could be in grave danger. When I asked what was in the package, she said it was better if I didn't know. At any rate, I told her I would do it."

"And when is she going to give you this package?"

"She said she didn't have it with her. But she's having it brought to her tonight."

"Are you going back there for dinner?"

"No, for lunch tomorrow. She has to go out tonight."

"Maybe to pick up the package?"

"Dunno."

15

At eight o'clock sharp he left the station and sped home to Marinella. The evening was more than perfect for eating outside. When he went to open the refrigerator, he froze.

Not because of what he saw inside, which he hadn't had the time even to take in, but because of what had unexpectedly flashed through his mind, stopping him dead in his tracks.

Where the hell was he keeping his head? What the hell was happening inside his brain?

Rhetorical questions, of course, since he knew perfectly well what was going on in his brain and where his head was: It was in Milan, with Marian.

And that was why he'd made a mistake as big as a house—actually, as big as a skyscraper.

So what could he do now to set things right? There was only one solution. To go personally in person.

He had to inform Marian at once. Upon hearing his voice, Marian sounded surprised.

"Ciao, Inspector. To what do I owe—"

"Sorry, I just wanted to say good night."

"Where are you?"

"At home, but I'm on my way out."

"Why, where are you going?"

"I've got some work to do tonight."

"What time will you be back?"

"I have no idea."

"So I can't call you later?"

"I don't think I'll be here."

"I'm sorry to hear that. Are you in a hurry?"

"Yes."

"Then till tomorrow, Inspector."

"Till tomorrow."

He prepared some coffee while hurriedly changing his clothes, putting on a pair of trousers with pockets all over, in which he put his cell phone, cigarettes, a book, a lighter, a flask of whisky, and a small thermos which he filled with the coffee he'd just made.

Then he donned a hunter's jacket and put a beret on his head and a pair of binoculars around his neck.

Then he made two sandwiches, one with salami and the other with provolone. Luckily Adelina had bought new provisions. He grabbed a half-bottle of wine and put everything in the pockets of the jacket.

He went out, got in the car, and drove back to Vigàta.

Destination: Via Palermo, number 28.

Valeria Bonifacio had said two important things to Augello: that she would be getting the package that night, and that she had to go out after dinner.

The easiest thing would have been to have her

followed and find out who she was meeting with. But he'd forgotten to give anyone this order, lost as he was in thoughts of Marian.

And so it was up to him to do what he'd neglected to tell someone else to do.

Via Palermo seemed to belong to another world. Indeed, one could park wherever one wanted. He pulled up right in front of her house, but on the opposite side of the street. There were two windows lit up, a sign that Valeria was still at home.

He pulled out a sandwich, the one with provolone, and started eating it. Instead of satisfying his appetite, it only made him hungrier. And so the salami sandwich met the same fate as its counterpart. He finished the wine and fired up a cigarette.

Some fifteen minutes later, seeing that nothing was happening, he started up the car and, in reverse, moved it under a streetlamp. From this position, the two windows were less visible and seen from the side, but still visible.

At half past eleven the two lights went out. He shut his book and set it down on the passenger's seat, ready to drive off.

Another ten minutes passed without anything happening. He started wondering whether Valeria might have gone to bed, in which case the whole thing would have been for naught. Or maybe she went to get her car. But where did she keep it?

He couldn't remember whether, when he'd gone to Bonifacio's house, he'd checked to see if there was a garage in back.

He saw a car come out from the street parallel to the house, but it was too dark to make out the person behind the wheel. Luckily at that moment another car drove by fast and lit up the first car for a moment with its headlights. There was no question: It was Valeria.

She drove slowly, making it easy for the inspector to follow her. If she started speeding there was no way he'd be able to keep up with her. Valeria took the Montereale road, driving past Marinella.

Hadn't De Nicola said that the call that Valeria had cut off came from the Montereale area?

But they didn't quite get to the town itself. About a quarter mile from the first houses, Valeria turned right onto a dirt road. It was a dark night, with almost no moonlight. Montalbano cursed the saints and, turning off his headlights, followed behind her, keeping a safe distance.

He couldn't see a thing and was afraid that at any moment he might end up in a gutter or ditch.

Suddenly he no longer saw the lights of Valeria's car. She'd stopped. It would have been too dangerous to get any closer in his car. She might hear it and get suspicious. He saw a sort of public fountain to his left and steered the car around and pulled up behind it. He locked the car and continued on foot.

After walking for about ten minutes he noticed a white glow up ahead. It was an open area in front of a stone quarry. Valeria had stopped her car there. He could see the red dots of her taillights.

At that moment he heard another car approaching. Montalbano quickly jumped off the road, hiding behind a large tree.

The second car went and pulled up alongside Valeria's. Meanwhile she'd gotten out of her car and was square in the path of the other car's headlights, which were promptly extinguished, though the driver left the parking lights on. There was now a man standing beside Valeria. They exchanged no greeting but immediately started talking. Montalbano could hear them but couldn't understand what they were saying.

They were two silhouettes whose faces remained indistinguishable. The man, however, must have been a good six feet tall. Montalbano tried his night binoculars, but they didn't help much.

His only option was to try to get closer, walking blindly in the dark and trying to make as little noise as possible. It wasn't easy, and he stumbled twice on tree roots and another time put his left foot in a deep hole full of water, soaking his leg to above the knee. All this without being able to curse the saints to let off steam.

At last he was able to make out a few phrases,

not because he'd come that much closer, but because the two had started raising their voices.

"But . . . what on earth . . . thinking?" said the man.

". . . listen . . . ," said Valeria.

"I wouldn't give it to you . . . even . . . rted crying."

"But don't you . . . ize that if . . . succeeds . . . and the police . . . find . . . Marta is fucked for . . . and you . . . free?"

"And if . . . doesn't? How can you . . . st this lawyer?"

". . . feel I . . . trust him."

"But who ca . . . you feel! My ass! Anyway, I . . . into the sea."

"I don't believe you."

"I'm telling you . . . I threw it into the sea."

At that moment Montalbano sneezed.

"What was that?" Valeria cried.

Montalbano sneezed again.

Without saying a word, the man was already in his car and driving away.

Sneeze number three.

Now it was Valeria who was running away. In the end fourteen straight sneezes left him in a daze. He must have inhaled some sort of pollen he was allergic to. Or maybe it was due to the liter of cold water he had in his left shoe. At least none of his men were around to see him make such an ass of himself. He walked back to his car and drove home. Clearly the man had not agreed to Valeria's plan. And he had no intention of giving her what she wanted. Or he could no longer give it to her. Something that could have fucked di Marta for good. But who was this man? Perhaps the same man Valeria hadn't wanted to talk to over the telephone?

And, speaking of telephones, how had Valeria managed to contact him and set up an appointment at the quarry? Clearly she'd used neither her cell phone nor her land line.

The first thing he did when he got to the office was call Officer De Nicola. This was not an easy task. He had to jump through numerous hoops, but in the end he got through to him.

"I'll take just a few seconds of your time. Did Signora Bonifacio either make or receive any phone calls from six-thirty onwards yesterday evening?"

"I think she made just one. If you can wait just a minute, I'll go and check."

"Please take your time and tell me what was said. I can wait."

He had to count up to 658.

"Hello?"

"I'm all ears, De Nicola."

"Signora Bonifacio called a certain Nina from her land line at six-fifty p.m., telling her she needed her because she'd had to invite some people to dinner at the last minute and needed Nina's help with the cooking. She had to insist because Nina didn't feel well. I also wanted to mention, sir, that at eight o'clock this morning she made a long call to a certain Diego, whose cell phone number is—"

"Never mind, that one's not important. Thanks."

Why had she called Mimì at eight o'clock? Maybe it was because the man she'd met the previous night hadn't agreed to do what she had in mind.

But the important thing was that the reason she'd given for needing this Nina was a lie. There hadn't been any dinner with guests, and therefore Nina's presence must have been needed for some other purpose. Perhaps they'd even spoken in code.

Mimì Augello showed up at half past nine, and to judge from his face, he looked rather crestfallen.

"She dumped me," he said, sitting down.

"Valeria dumped you?"

"She called me at eight this morning and kept me on for half an hour. She said our affair ended here and she didn't feel like taking it any further, she couldn't do that to her husband, she was an honest woman, after all . . . She was so convincing, I very nearly thought she was telling the truth. At any rate, there was no changing her mind."

"Mimì, I think you're losing your touch, if women are starting to ditch you at the first opportunity," said the inspector, just to be an asshole.

"I guess I am," Mimì assented disconsolately.

"Good morning, everyone," Fazio said, entering.

"Have you heard the news?" Montalbano asked him. "Valeria doesn't want anything more to do with our good Inspector Augello."

"And why not?"

Mimì was about to reply, but the inspector raised his hand to stop him.

"I'll answer that question."

"I'd rather you didn't," said Mimì.

"Why?"

"Because you just like to make fun of me."

"I assure you the explanation is entirely in your favor."

"Okay, then, let's hear it."

"Valeria broke up with the Don Juan here present because she was never given the package she was supposed to hand over to him."

"And how do you know that?" asked Mimì.

Montalbano recounted the whole story of his adventure of the previous night, leaving out the minor detail of his sneezing. The immediate effect was to bring a smile back to Augello's face.

"So she dumped me because she didn't need me anymore."

"And not because your manly gifts were wanting," said Montalbano. "You can take comfort."

And he continued:

"I want you to try to remember something, Mimì: Did Valeria ever happen to mention a certain Nina to you?"

"Nina? No, never," said Augello.

"Maybe it's the name of her cleaning lady," a pensive Fazio cut in.

"Look into it. Meanwhile, have you found out anything new?"

"Not much. This Valeria naturally has many acquaintances, but only one true friend, Loredana. If she ever goes to the movies, it's always with her. If she has to go to Montelusa to buy herself a dress or a pair of good shoes, she goes with her friend. They are never apart. They're like Siamese twins."

"No men?"

"An elderly lady—but one with good vision—who lives in the house almost directly across from her and sits at her window in a wheelchair all day every day told me that until about two months ago, a man would come and visit Valeria three times a week, always in the afternoon. Then, about two months ago, he stopped coming and hasn't been seen since. According to her, they had a quarrel, a nasty one. When the man was leaving, the last time he came, Valeria stuck her head out the window and started yelling obscenities at him and told him never to come back."

"And how old was this man?" asked Montalbano.

"Maybe twenty-five, max."

"Maybe a lover," Augello commented.

"I asked the old lady," said Fazio. "She said she didn't think so."

"How could she possibly know? It's not as if she can see all the way inside their house, is it?"

"No, but sometimes Valeria would come out with him and walk him to his car. According to the woman, they didn't say good-bye the way lovers do."

"Then maybe he's a relative," said Augello.

"She doesn't have any. No brothers or sisters, no cousins."

"What strikes me most," said Montalbano, "is the regularity."

"In what sense?" asked Augello.

"That he went there three times a week and always in the afternoon. It's a kind of standing appointment."

He paused, then looked at Fazio.

"Did she tell what days of the week?"

"Yes, Mondays, Wednesdays, and Fridays."

He had an idea.

"Can you go back and talk to her again?"

"Sure."

"Ask her whether Loredana was also there when

this man came to Valeria's, and explain to her what she looks like."

He turned to Augello and continued:

"Mimì, I still need your brazen face."

"What for?"

"Starting this morning, Loredana will reopen the supermarket, which has been closed because there's been nobody to manage it, and she'll probably be filling in for her husband. So starting now, she'll have to be there mornings and afternoons."

"So?"

"So you have to go and talk to her."

"On what pretext?"

"Tell her that you're desperate, that you want to kill yourself, that you realize that without Valeria, you're finished, ruined. And ask her to intervene on your behalf."

"And what if she says no?"

"If she says no, you've at least established a relationship with Loredana. It's better than nothing."

"I'll go there now."

"No, it's too early, let her get oriented first. Show up there around four, in tears, when the store reopens. And we'll all meet back here at five. Let's go, guys, the solution may be just around the corner."

As soon as he sat down on the flat rock after having eaten and drunk, he noticed that this time there were two crabs waiting there for him. Maybe they were brothers.

Valeria has no brothers or sisters.

Maybe the crabs were brother and sister. How do you tell a male crab from a female crab?

As he was tossing little sea pebbles at the crabs, a thought whirled around inside his head.

It was something that someone had said concerning Valeria. Something that at the time hadn't seemed important to him. But maybe it was. The problem was that he couldn't bring it into focus.

Fazio and Augello came in punctually at five.

"You talk first, Mimì."

"Loredana immediately remembered me. I was able to talk to her for barely ten minutes in the manager's office. She said she knew about me and Valeria because her friend had told her about it in great detail. She even said that it was the first time since Valeria got married that she was interested in another man. I went into hysterics and even started crying. She took pity on me and said she would talk to Valeria."

"So how did you leave things with her?"

"She wanted my cell phone number. She's gonna get back to me on it."

"And what about you?" Montalbano asked, turning to Fazio.

"I talked to the old lady. You were right on

the money, Chief. Whenever that man came, Loredana was always there."

"Did you ask her what he looked like?"

"The young guy? Yes, she said he was a good six feet tall and always came in the same car."

"Did she remember any part of the license plate number or the make of car?"

"No, Chief, she didn't get a look at the license plate and doesn't know the first thing about car models. All she said was that the car was silver."

"I'm almost certain that the guy's car the other night was also silver," said Montalbano. "But there's no question it's the same guy who used to go and see her at home. Unless all the men Valeria frequents are six feet tall."

"I found out something else," Fazio went on. "That her cleaning lady's name is Nina. But she's not really a proper cleaning lady; she was Valeria's wet nurse when her mother stopped producing milk because of some unpleasantness."

"And who told you all this?"

"The only greengrocer in all of Via Palermo, where Nina does her shopping."

Hearing this story about Valeria's mother losing her milk because of an unpleasant misfortune brought back to Montalbano's mind the thing that had occurred to him when he was sitting on the flat rock.

And he suddenly remembered that it was Augello who'd said this important thing.

"Mimì, if I remember correctly, when you came and told us about your first encounter with Valeria, I think you said that she'd told you her life story."

"That's right."

"I can't quite remember now, but didn't you say she talked about her family?"

"Yes, she said she'd had an unhappy childhood because her father had a mistress with whom he had a son."

"Okay, that was it. Did she tell you whether this son was born before her?"

"Yes, four years before."

"So Valeria has a half-brother."

"Well, if that's the case . . ."

"Did she tell you whether her father ever acknowledged paternity?"

"No, she didn't."

Fazio was already standing up.

"I'm gonna dash over to the records office. Our computer system is down. The office closes at five-thirty. Maybe I can still make it."

16

"I don't understand why you think this half-brother is so important," said Mimì Augello.

"Mimì, it is crystal clear that Valeria leads a double life. Or, at least there's a large part of her life she now wants to keep hidden at all costs. Do you agree?"

"I agree."

"If the scheme of the package she wanted to give you had gone according to plan, by now we would surely have discovered something. But since things didn't go as expected, we still know nothing at our end of things. But all roads are viable. It's possible that she and the half-brother have continued to meet."

They kept talking about Valeria until Fazio returned, discomfited, half an hour later.

"All I found at city hall was that there's only one male Bonifacio in Vigàta, Vittorio, who's fifty years old and is Valeria's father. Therefore Vittorio did not acknowledge paternity for his illegitimate son, who must be registered under his mother's maiden name."

"Speaking of mothers, what is Valeria's mother's maiden name?" asked Montalbano. "Maybe through her . . ."

"Her name was Agata Tessitore. She died three years ago."

"We've reached a dead end," Mimì commented.

But the inspector had already clamped his teeth around the bone and wasn't about to let go.

"Okay, I'm going to make a desperate move," he said. "But I should let you know that it worked once before."

He dialed a number on the outside line and turned on the speakerphone.

"Hello?" answered a woman's voice.

"Adelì, this is Montalbano here."

"Ah, so iss you, Isspector? Wha'ss wrong? Everyting okay?"

"I need a little information. Do you know an elderly woman who keeps house for a certain young woman with the surname of Bonifacio?"

"No, sir."

"This elderly woman's name is Nina."

"Nina Bonsignori?"

"I don't know her surname."

"I know an ol' leddy who buys a fish atta semma place I buy itta masself, anna she alway talkin' about 'er boss, always a talkin' my ear offa tellin' whatta goo' younga leddy she is anna so beauty-full. She sez she raise her, an' she wazza her wet nurse . . ."

Bull's-eye.

"That's the one!"

And after casting a triumphant glance at Mimì and Fazio, he continued:

"And is her boss's name Valeria?"

"Yessir."

"When are you going to see Nina again?"

"I'm a sure am a gonna see her tomorra mornin' azza usual, a' seven-thirty atta fish market."

"Okay, now I'm going to tell you what I want you to ask her, but you should do it offhandedly, as if it's just out of curiosity. And when you have her answer, I want you to call me at home."

"It canna wait till I comma to you house?"

"No, I have to know right away."

After hanging up, he turned to Fazio and said:

"Tomorrow morning, as soon as I have this woman's name, I'm going to call you with it, and I want you to run immediately to the records office."

He got home just before eight-thirty, and the moment he entered the phone rang.

"Hello, Salvo."

It was Livia. She spoke slowly, in a faint, faraway voice, as if it cost her great effort to breathe.

"Hi. Are you feeling any better?"

"No. Worse. Today I couldn't even manage to go to work. I stayed home."

"But are you sick? Do you have any fever?"

"No, no fever. But it's as if I did."

"Can't you explain any better what—"

"Salvo, I'm living with a sense of continuous, piercing anguish inside me. However hard I try—and, believe me, I do try—I can't find the cause of it. But there it is. It's as if something really terrible was about to happen to me at any moment."

Montalbano felt very bad about this.

He imagined her there alone, disheveled, eyes red with tears, walking gloomily from room to room . . . The next words came straight from his heart:

"Listen . . . Do you want me to come to Boccadasse?"

"No."

"Maybe I could help you."

"No."

"Why?"

"I would be impossible."

"But you can't just stay like that without doing anything!"

"If I still feel like this tomorrow, I'll go and see someone. I promise. But now I need to sleep."

"I hope you can."

"With sleeping pills I can. Good night."

He had a bitter taste in his mouth, and a heavy heart.

He sat down in the armchair and turned on the television. Zito was just ending his report.

". . . for the investigating magistrate, Antonio Grasso, today was the deadline for confirming or dismissing the arrest of Salvatore di Marta, but Judge Grasso has requested an additional forty-eight hours before deciding. We can therefore infer that the evidence the prosecutor's office considered sufficient for issuing the arrest warrant was deemed not quite as convincing and certain by the investigating magistrate.

"Elsewhere in the news, the hunt for three immigrants after an exchange of gunfire with law enforcement officials a few days ago continues in the Raccadali countryside. An abandoned farmhouse has been discovered in which the three men are believed to have temporarily taken shelter. Bloodied rags have been found there, confirming the report that one of them had been seriously wounded. Commissioner Sposìto, head of the counterterrorism unit of Montelusa and its province, says that the ring around the three fugitives is tightening and that their capture and arrest is now just a question of time.

"In other news, we have just learned that the municipal council of . . ."

He started changing channels, looking for a movie. He didn't feel the least bit hungry. Livia's phone call had killed his appetite. He found a spy movie and watched it till the end, even though he didn't understand a thing.

He turned off the TV and went and sat down on the veranda. He didn't even feel like any whisky. He felt melancholy about Livia.

He started thinking of her again at home in Boccadasse. The sorrow, tenderness, and compassion he felt for her brought a lump to his throat.

And he saw himself reflected in her, since she was suffering from the same loneliness he had felt before meeting Marian.

Maybe Livia had been right to refuse his offer to come to Boccadasse. What comfort could he really have given her? Would he have been able to hold her and caress her the way he used to do?

Maybe with words? But not only would his words not have been up to the challenge, they would have rung false. Because you can't live with a person for years on end, get to know him inside and out, and not notice when something changes inside this person. And Livia had surely already noticed the change in him.

But this time she hadn't reacted. On the contrary, she'd made a point of saying that her malaise had nothing to do with their relationship.

So what could have happened to her? What was the cause of this anguish that had suddenly overwhelmed her? Was it some bad joke of advancing age?

What he found most disturbing was the fact that Livia was not prone to hysteria or sudden fits of depression, or wild fantasies or mood shifts. On the contrary. She had a gift for concreteness, for having both feet always on the ground. If she was feeling this way now, the reason must be very serious. And the situation could become more dangerous if they didn't soon find the cause.

No, he couldn't possibly abandon her at such a moment. It would be an act of twofold cowardice.

Almost as if she'd heard him thinking, Marian called. That is, as the phone was ringing, he was absolutely certain that it was Marian at the other end. Reaching out for the phone cost him a great deal of effort, and the receiver seemed to weigh a ton.

"Hello . . . who is this?"

"Ciao, Inspector, how are you? Your voice sounds strange."

"I'm . . . tired. Very tired."

"Last night must have tired you out."

"Yes. It was . . . rough. How are things with you?"

"Lariani was very mysterious the last time we spoke on the phone. He said he had to be extremely cautious with the people he was dealing with. When I asked him why, he didn't answer. He still needs another day."

"And what did you say?"

"I granted him the extra day. But I made a

decision. I'm giving him until tomorrow evening. If he doesn't get in touch, or if he puts it off again, that's it."

"What do you mean?"

"I mean that's it, I'm dropping everything."

"Are you serious?"

"Of course I'm serious."

"But isn't this a good opportunity?"

"It certainly is!"

"So why drop something when you're already almost there?"

"Salvo, perhaps you still don't understand."

"Understand what?"

"That being one minute, even one minute away from you costs me a great deal. And being a whole day away is too high a price. A price I can no longer pay. And there's nothing whatsoever forcing me to subject myself to such suffering. To hell with Pedicini, Lariani, and the rest. They're all thieves!"

"What are you saying?"

"Yes, thieves! They've robbed me of a piece of happiness. And my happiness comes before anything else. Have I made myself clear?"

Before answering, he had to let a few seconds pass. He felt bowled over by Marian's stridency.

"You've made yourself perfectly clear," he finally said.

But a question kept spinning around in his head: Why was Lariani acting this way?

"Now," Marian resumed in the same tone as before, "since I'm convinced by now that nothing will be resolved by the end of the day tomorrow, I'm going to catch a flight early the following day and come back to Vigàta. That way, we can be together for dinner in the evening."

"I can understand your reasons, but just think it over, please, since you're about to seal the deal—after all, one day more or one day less . . . ," said Montalbano *cunctator*, the procrastinator.

Marian raised her voice.

"Salvo, I will not allow them to steal, to rob me of another second of my time with you. Can't you get that through your head? Don't you start now too. Anyway, don't delude yourself: Now that I've got you, I'm not about to let you go."

He'd never heard her sound so determined.

"All right," he said.

Marian changed tone.

"I'm sorry if . . . But I feel exasperated. I'm just boiling inside. I've thought about this long and hard. I was a fool to accept Pedicini's proposal. I should have said no even if it only involved being away for a single day."

"But now you should calm down," said Montalbano. "Otherwise you won't sleep a wink."

"I have a remedy for that."

"You really shouldn't take sleeping pills, which—"

"I have no intention of taking sleeping pills. You are my sleeping pill."

"Me?"

"Yes, you're my stimulant and my sedative. Wish me good night, as if I were lying beside you."

"Good night," said Montalbano, truly wishing that Marian were lying beside him.

He had just come out of the shower at quarter past eight when the telephone rang.

"Isspecter, 'iss Adelina."

"What is it, Adelì?"

"I talk a witta Nina Bonsignori. An' ya kenna stoppa that leddy when she start a talk abou' her boss, 'oo even called onna sill phone when she was tellin' me everyting."

"Nina has a cell phone?"

"Yessir, evverybaddy gotta sill phone now."

"Go on."

"She tol' me the name o' the lover o' her bossa father, an' iss Francesca Lauricella."

As soon as he hung up, he rang Fazio and told him about the phone call.

As he was about to go out, he dialed Livia's number. She answered with a thick tongue.

"What time is it?"

"Nine. Sorry if I woke you up."

"I wasn't asleep. But I'm still in bed and don't feel like getting up. Why did you call?"

"To see how you were. I'm worried."

"I'm the same. But you shouldn't worry. Please. Let's talk again tonight."

What heartache he felt upon talking to her! And how stingy he'd become, how few words of sincerity and generosity he had for her!

To go to the station he had no choice but to drive past Marian's gallery. This time he noticed that some asshole had written "THIEVES!" in green and red spray paint on the metal shutter. It served as an arbitrary reminder that Marian had used the same word for Lariani. He wished he could meet the guy. But there was another way to find out more about him. Why hadn't he thought of it sooner? Damn the condition his head was in!

Fazio and Mimì were waiting for him at the office.

"So?"

Fazio pulled a piece of paper out of his pocket. The inspector warned him:

"I realize that the public record is important in this case, but spare me the rosary. Just give me the kid's name."

"His name is Rosario Lauricella, and he's twenty-five years old," Fazio said stiffly, putting the piece of paper back in his pocket.

"Where does he live?"

"In Montereale. And I can even tell you that on

his ID card he measures one meter and eighty-one centimeters. And there's more."

"You can tell me later. First I want to call Tommaseo to tell him I no longer need a tap on Valeria's and Loredana's phones."

"Wait," said Fazio. "What if Valeria happens to call Rosario?"

"She won't. I've figured out how she communicates with him."

"How?"

"With her cleaning lady's cell phone. That's what she did the night of their meeting at the quarry. And to talk to Loredana, she can now go and see her in person."

He called Tommaseo, then let Fazio have his say.

"Chief, I don't know this Rosario in person but I know who he is."

"And who is he?"

"The Cuffaro family's representative in Montereale. He might be young, but they really trust him."

This was unexpected. The inspector just stared at Fazio openmouthed.

Then he pulled himself together.

"But it doesn't seem possible that Savastano's murder was a Mafia hit!"

"Why not?" Augello cut in. "Just because Guttadauro said it wasn't? He was probably just pulling your leg."

Montalbano shook his head pensively.

"No," he said at last. "I'm convinced Guttadauro was sincere."

"And so?"

The inspector remained silent. Then he stood up and, with his eyes looking past everyone in the room at some faraway point in space, he went over to the window, came back, sat down, and finally declared in a calm voice to the two men looking at him in puzzlement:

"Guys, I've figured it all out."

"Well, if you feel like letting us in on it too . . ." said Mimì.

"Let me start with a disclaimer. The reconstruction I am about to present has no evidence whatsoever to back it up, only logic. And it begins with my sincere belief that after Loredana married di Marta, Carmelo Savastano kept on bothering the girl, but she said nothing to her husband, fearing his reaction."

"You mean he wanted to sleep with her?" Mimì asked.

"Maybe. Or, more precisely, he wished. But I'm convinced that he mostly blackmailed her into giving him money. In all likelihood he never turned over all the footage he'd filmed. Remember when di Marta told us that at one point he wanted her to prostitute herself with somebody? Maybe it really happened, and Savastano caught it on film. And naturally Valeria, her bosom friend, would know all about this. Every so often, Rosario Lauricella, Valeria's half-brother, comes to see her, and sometimes Loredana's there. And Rosario and the girl end up falling in love and become lovers. Valeria makes a room available to them, and the two get together on Mondays, Wednesdays, and Fridays. At a certain point, however, Rosario finds out about Loredana's situation with Savastano. And I think it was Valeria who told him."

"Why Valeria?" asked Fazio.

"Because I consider her the smartest of them all, and I think that she already had her plan in mind when she spoke with her brother. Which was to free herself, in one fell swoop, of both Savastano and di Marta. Before putting her plan into effect, Valeria takes the precaution of making it look like she's had a falling-out with Rosario. She appears to have broken off all relations with him. And she's so careful that, knowing he works for the Cuffaros, she uses her cleaning lady's cell phone when she needs to talk to him."

"Didn't I tell you the girl was a master?" said Mimì.

"So, to come to the point, on the evening when Loredana goes to Valeria's house and tells her she has sixteen thousand euros in her purse, Valeria calls her cleaning lady and tells her to call Rosario and tell him to go to Via Palermo at once. Rosario drives off from Montereale, leaves the car nearby, and goes a short distance on foot, making sure nobody sees him. At that moment his only assignment is to grab the money and have rough sex with Loredana, leaving visible marks on her body. You know the rest. The upshot is that we all end up thinking that Savastano was somehow involved, especially di Marta, who will thus become the prime suspect in a murder that has yet to happen."

"Okay, now to part two," said Mimì.

"When Loredana informs Valeria that she's told her husband her attacker was Savastano, Valeria contacts Rosario, who's surely been having Savastano followed for some time. Rosario, together with an accomplice, lies in wait for Savastano outside the gambling joint he often frequents, they kidnap him, take him out to the country, shoot him, and set the car on fire. They want to make it look like a Mafia hit, but this proves to be a miscalculation, since the Mafia make it clear they're on the sidelines."

"And what about the famous package?" Augello asked.

"I'll explain. Valeria realizes there's no proof that di Marta did it. She needs to give us some, but it has to be bomb-proof proof. So she thinks of asking Rosario for the gun he used to kill Savastano, so she can wipe away the fingerprints, put it in a box, and give it to you, Mimì."

"And what was I supposed to do with it?"

"Hide it somewhere in di Marta's office in the supermarket and then send us an anonymous letter. Whereupon we would search the office and find it. Which would have screwed di Marta forever. But Rosario isn't convinced, and on top of that, he says he threw the gun into the sea. Which I think is true. I don't think he's stupid enough to keep the gun."

"Well, that's a very fine novel you just recounted to us," said Augello. "But how are we going to make it become a reality?"

"That is the question," said Montalbano. "For the moment, at least, I haven't the slightest idea. Let's meet again later, because now, if you'll allow me, I have a personal phone call to make."

With Fazio and Mimì out of the office, he rang the central police headquarters of Milan and, after identifying himself, asked to speak with Deputy Commissioner Attilio Strazzeri. He and Strazzeri had long remained friends after their time at the academy together, and the inspector had once done him a big favor. He was now hoping Strazzeri still remembered.

"Hey, Salvo, what a pleasure! Long time no see! How are you?"

"Not too bad. And yourself?"

"Pretty good, thanks. You need something?"

"Attì, are you by any chance friends with the person in charge there of art theft, art forgeries, and stuff like that?"

"Very good friends, actually. More than a brother. I am he in the flesh."

Montalbano heaved a sigh of relief. With Strazzeri he could speak openly.

17

"I want to know something about an art dealer, assuming you've heard of him. His name is Gianfranco Lariani."

There was no answer.

"Hello?" said the inspector.

Not a breath at the other end. Overcome by a fit of separation anxiety, Montalbano started to panic and began yelling like a madman.

"Hello? Is anyone there? Hello!"

"What's got into you?" said Strazzeri. "I'm right here."

"Then why don't you answer?"

"Because your question caught me by surprise."

And what was so surprising about it?

"But do you know the man? Yes or no?"

"Listen, Salvo, write down this number. It's my cell phone number. And call me back in five minutes."

He wrote down the number. He felt a bit unsettled by Strazzeri's strange reaction. Then he dialed the number.

"Montalbano here."

"Sorry, Salvo, but there were some people in the room. Now I'm alone and can talk. Yes, I know Lariani. What did you want to know?"

"If he can be counted on."

Strazzeri started laughing.

"Hell, yes! Absolutely! He was arrested some years ago and convicted. And he's a repeat offender. His specialty is exporting stolen artworks."

The entire world, with all its oceans and continents, and the men and beasts inhabiting them, came crashing down on Montalbano's head. An ice-cold sweat covered him from the roots of his hair to the tips of his toes. He wanted to speak but couldn't.

"Hello? Are you there?" asked Strazzeri this time.

"Yes," the inspector struggled to say. "And how . . . how does he do it?"

"How does he export them? By a variety of methods. The most brilliant one is using a double canvas. A canvas of decent, exportable value is used to cover the stolen canvas that is classified as part of the national cultural heritage."

It was ninety-nine percent certain that the painting Lariani was going to turn over to Marian was rigged in this way. She, poor thing, completely unaware, would pay for it and take it to Pedicini, who would then load it on his boat, and that would be the last she'd ever see of him.

"We've been keeping an eye on him for a while," Strazzeri continued. "We think he's planning a major coup. He's usually in cahoots with an accomplice whose job is to win the trust of a dealer, collector, or small-town gallerist, and then—"

"Pedicini?"

Dead silence. Menaced again by a fear of abandonment, the inspector started yelling desperately before Strazzeri spoke up.

"Oh, no you don't! You're not playing straight with me! My dear friend and colleague, you call me up after years of silence, and just like that you come out with the names of Lariani and Pedicini? I think you must have something important to tell me. I told you what you wanted to know, and now it's your turn to speak."

Montalbano weighed his options. In a flash he became convinced that the only way to get Marian out of this pickle was to have her collaborate with Strazzeri. In exchange he could ask his friend to keep her name out of this.

"And what if I bring you Lariani's head on a platter?" he asked. "Think we can make a deal?"

"Speak," replied Strazzeri.

He told him the whole story. They made an agreement. And in the end Strazzeri told him what he had to do.

He immediately rang Marian.

"Salvo, what's wrong?" she asked in alarm.

"What's wrong is that you were about to get mixed up in a great big scam. Lariani is a crook, he's already done jail time."

"Oh my God!"

"Now listen to me. I'm going to give you a telephone number. It's for the office of Attilio Strazzeri, deputy police commissioner of the City of Milan, a trusted friend of mine. You must call him the minute you get off the phone with me and make yourself available to him. Got that?"

"But what will they do with me?"

Her voice was quavering; she was starting to cry.

"They won't do anything with you. They're not going to arrest you, and your name will be kept out of the whole thing, don't worry. All you need to do is meet with Strazzeri and do what he asks you to do. I send you a kiss. Call him right now. And ring me tonight. Take down this number."

He dictated it to her, had her repeat it back to him, then hung up. He felt a little better now.

He felt an overwhelming need to go outside and walk, to get over the fright he'd just had. But first he dropped into Fazio's office.

"Summon Valeria Bonifacio for four-thirty this afternoon. And inform Augello. We'll all meet back up in my office at four."

He left his car in the parking lot and started walking randomly, with no precise destination. It occurred to him he'd never wandered about the streets in town like this at that hour of the morning. He stopped in front of the most elegant men's clothing store in Vigàta. He needed a few shirts, but the prices on the ones displayed in the window chased him away.

All at once he found himself in front of the metal shutter of the gallery with the word "THIEVES!" written on it. He stared at it.

If not for that graffiti . . .

A municipal cop he knew pulled up beside him.

"You know what, Inspector? This morning we nabbed the guy who was going around mucking everything up with green spray paint."

"Oh, yeah? And who was it?"

"Some poor bastard half out of his mind. His name is Ernesto Lo Vullo. He mucked up half the buildings in town, the façade of the church, the monument to the fallen . . ."

"And what are you going to do with him?"

"He'll either have to pay a fine of three hundred and fifty euros or we'll press charges and he'll do a few days in the slammer. Where's he going to find that kind of money? The guy's a down-and-outer who's panhandling half the time."

Montalbano said good-bye to the beat cop and dashed into the town hall, asking directions for the office he wanted. Then, before the astonished, spellbound eyes of the clerk, he paid Ernesto Lo Vullo's fine with a check, and then resumed his walk.

He stopped to look into the window of a store called Vigàta Elettronica. On display were various computers and things called iPods, iPads, and iPuds, as well as recorders that looked like cell phones.

As he was looking at the latter, he thought of a way to corner Valeria Bonifacio.

He went inside and bought one of the gadgets. The salesman wanted to explain how it worked, but Montalbano told him not to bother, since at any rate he wouldn't have understood a thing even if the inventor himself explained it to him. He also told him he didn't need the box, and he slipped the thing into his coat pocket along with the instruction booklet. He paid and decided it was time to go to the trattoria.

At Enzo's he was sure he'd done the right thing, but until the whole case was wrapped up he couldn't be sure of anything. He wanted to call Marian, but was afraid that his phone call would interrupt her at the wrong moment. He would have given the world to be beside her just then.

He came out of the restaurant at three, but didn't feel like taking his usual walk along the jetty. He'd already walked enough, so he went back to the station.

Stopping in front of Catarella, he pulled out the recorder he'd bought.

"Do you know how to make this thing work?"

"Assolutely, Chief."

"And what do you do to listen to the recording?"

"Y'either load it onna yer kapewter or eltz ya need 'eadphones, Chief."

The salesman hadn't said anything about head-phones.

"Could you go and buy me a pair at the store called Vigàta Elettronica?"

Catarella looked at his watch.

"It'll reopen in half an hour."

"How much do they cost?"

"Toity euros oughter be anuff. I'll get the best."

"I want them by four-fifteen at the latest," said Montalbano, giving him the money.

The meeting with Augello and Fazio started at four o'clock sharp. It was up to Montalbano to do the talking.

"Listen to me carefully. I've decided to set a trap for La Bonifacio. It's our only chance to get her to betray herself. The trap will unfold in three separate moves. First move: Valeria gets here and finds me here with Fazio. I talk to her, and five minutes later we make the second move. Which is that you, Mimì, will knock and come in. And I'll introduce you as Deputy Inspector Augello. We'll talk about the package. She'll say she wanted to surprise you and that the package was only to contain a little present. And at this point I'll make the third move."

"And what's that?"

"I'm not going to tell you."

"Why not?"

"Because in my opinion it's better if you both react spontaneously."

The office door flew open, striking the wall with a bomblike crash.

"My 'and slipped," said an embarrassed Catarella, frozen in the doorway.

Fazio gave him a dirty look, while Montalbano glared at him in anger and Augello's eyes shot lightning bolts at him.

Paralyzed by all these eyes, Catarella, who had a box in his hand, didn't move.

"Come on in."

"The he . . . he . . . he . . ."

"Put 'em on the desk and get out of here."

Montalbano opened the box, pulled out the headset, tore off the cellophane wrapping, stuck the set in a drawer, and tossed the box into the wastebasket.

"It's for the trap," he explained.

"I want to know exactly when I'm supposed to enter," said Augello.

"Mimì, as soon as Catarella tells us Valeria is here, you're going to go into your office, count up to five hundred, and then come and knock at my door."

The telephone rang.

"Chief, 'ere'd be a Signura Benefaccio onna premisses."

"It's her, she's early," said Montalbano.

Mimì got up and disappeared.

"Show her in."

Valeria was in fine form. She was all spiffed up and made up and decked out, with a big smile on her face. But despite her efforts not to let it show, the anxiety over having been called in must have been eating away at her.

"Please sit down, signora," said the inspector.

Valeria sat down at the edge of the chair, and smiled even at Fazio. Then she gave Montalbano a questioning glance, tilting her head slightly to one side. She was a picture of innocence personified.

"As perhaps you already know, since the investigating magistrate has failed to confirm the arrest of Salvatore di Marta, the public prosecutor has requested further investigation. Personally I don't think there's anything more to discover; it's all pretty clear by now, but we still have to carry out our orders."

Valeria visibly relaxed and settled more comfortably into her chair.

"I've already told you everything I had to say," she said.

"I don't doubt it. You've been honest and straightforward with me, and I shall do the same for you. You can answer my questions without fear."

"Okay."

"Do you know a lawyer by the name of Diego Croma?"

Valeria's entire body shook, as if from an electric shock, but she quickly recovered.

"Yes, but I don't see what that—"

With perfect timing, as if they'd rehearsed the scene all afternoon, there was a knock at the door.

"Come in," said the inspector.

Mimì Augello entered smiling. It was impressive to see just how much the expression on Valeria's face changed. In an instant she became surly, dark, and suspicious, as she struggled to understand what the lawyer's presence there might mean.

"Allow me to introduce Inspector Augello," said Montalbano.

Valeria's reaction took them all by surprise. She started smiling again.

"Hi. What need was there to present yourself under a false name? I would have liked you even if you were a cop."

Mimì, confused, said nothing. Montalbano, in his head, couldn't help but tip his hat to her. What a woman! What exceptional self-control! You really had to watch your step with someone like her.

"Could you please tell me what was supposed to be in the package you intended to give to Inspector Augello, and which he was supposed to hide in an unspecified place in turn?"

Valeria laughed.

"But what are you thinking! It was supposed to

contain a small necklace. I wanted to surprise Loredana and have her discover it in the manager's office at the supermarket."

"Why did you change your mind?"

"Because I wanted nothing more to do with this Diego Croma, or Inspector Augello—I don't even know what to call him anymore. Our friendship had taken an overly . . . well, intimate turn, and I decided to break things off."

Montalbano had been expecting this explanation. All that was left now was to make the third move, the decisive one.

"Signora, we have information that the other evening, after midnight, you met with a man."

"I haven't gone out at night for months."

"Signora, you should know that your telephones have been under surveillance for several days, and that—"

Valeria swallowed this like a piece of candy.

"Then I challenge you to let me hear the phone call in which I supposedly made an appointment with this hypothetical—"

"I can't let you hear it because you used your cleaning woman's cell phone to make that call."

The shot was on the mark, but Valeria could take her hits like a pro and return fire at once.

"You dreamed that up, it's not true. Anyway, my cleaning woman would never admit it, not even under torture, even if it were true."

"I'm telling you we know with absolute certainty that you met with a man."

"Well, even if I did, I don't think that's a crime. I also met with the man who called himself Diego Croma. Isn't that right, counsel?"

"No, it's not a crime. Not at all. But I'd like to ask you a question. Do you remember why you and the man you met were suddenly forced to interrupt your conversation at the rock quarry and hurry back to your respective cars?"

"How could I possibly remember if I wasn't there?"

"Then allow me to refresh your memory. Someone nearby sneezed."

Valeria blanched. Fazio and Augello looked at each other in confusion. Montalbano continued.

"That someone was me. I sneezed fourteen times in a row. Would you like to hear me?"

He pulled the recorder out of his pocket and set it on the desk, then opened a drawer and withdrew the headset, which he offered to Valeria.

"Before the series of sneezes you'll also be able to hear, in this recording, your entire conversation with the man. You wanted the pistol with which the man murdered Carmelo Savastano, in accordance with the plan you devised, so you could put it in a box and have the here-present Inspector Augello hide it in the management office of the supermarket. Once it was found, Signor di Marta would most certainly have been convicted."

Valeria didn't move. She'd become a statue of white plaster. A mildly quaking statue, that is.

"Naturally," the inspector continued, "we've identified the man. His name is Rosario Lauricella, your half-brother and Loredana di Marta's lover. You generously lent them the use of a room in your house for their thrice-weekly appointments. And it was in this room that the phony rape of Loredana was performed."

Valeria was like a bowstring tensed to the point of spasm. The inspector decided to let her spring.

"But you know what? Rosario lied to you. He told you he'd got rid of the gun by throwing it into the sea, but in fact this wasn't true. We found it at his home a couple of hours ago, when we went to arrest him. In the face of such obvious and overwhelming proof, he broke down and confessed. He said it was you who organized everything. And therefore I here—"

He was unable to finish his sentence.

Valeria leapt up from her chair and tried to scratch his face, wielding her fingers like claws. Montalbano stepped aside as Fazio and Augello grabbed her on the fly.

"That stupid asshole! That imbecile! I told him to give *me* the pistol! But all the guy knows how to do is kill and fuck! And now he's screwed us all!"

She was blindly kicking the air like a mule.

Mimì was put out of commission by a kick in the giggleberries.

Hearing all the racket, Gallo and another cop came running and finally managed to restrain the young woman.

They took her into a holding cell foaming at the mouth, cursing like a demon in hell and accusing Loredana of having organized the whole plot.

Fazio, Augello, and Montalbano himself took a good fifteen minutes to put his office back in order after it had been turned upside down by Valeria's fury.

"Congratulations," said Augello.

"All the same," said Fazio, "I can understand Loredana's interests in this affair, and I can understand Rosario's interests. What I can't understand is what interest Valeria could have had in what they did."

"Me neither, as far as that goes," said Augello.

"Well, for one thing," said Montalbano, "there's a financial interest. With di Marta convicted, Loredana would have become practically the sole heir of his wealth. And she would have richly rewarded her bosom friend for organizing the brilliant scheme to liberate her from her husband, making her rich and freeing her up for a life of bliss with her lover. And I'm convinced that Valeria's feeling of friendship for Loredana bordered on passionate love. She only hated di Marta because he'd nabbed Loredana by buying her. She knew that Loredana was suffering with a husband so much older than her. She was ready to do anything just to make her happy. But I don't think she'll ever confess to these things."

"Speaking of which," said Fazio, "when should we put the confession down on record?"

"Go and talk to her right now," said Montalbano. "You go, too, Mimì. If we leave her too much time to calm down and start thinking, she's likely to deal from a different deck. Then you, Mimì, go to Tommaseo, give him the written confession, and get him to give you an arrest warrant for Loredana and another for Rosario Lauricella."

"Montereale's not in our jurisdiction," Augello pointed out.

"Then pass it on to the Flying Squad or the Catturandi. See what Tommaseo tells you."

Fazio and Augello left. The inspector looked at his watch. Five-thirty. A record.

What was Marian doing at that moment?

He waited until nine o'clock, feeling more and more agitated. Why was there no word from Mimì or Fazio? And what if in the meanwhile Marian had tried to call him at home and hadn't found him?

Had Tommaseo perhaps put up some obstacle?

The first to return was Augello.

"Tommaseo was great. He didn't waste a single minute. He issued the two arrest warrants immediately, and Fazio said he'd go and arrest Loredana himself. I lent the Flying Squad a hand."

"Did you catch Rosario?"

"No. The general impression is that he's gone into hiding."

"One possible explanation is that Valeria tipped him off with her cleaning lady's cell phone, telling him she'd been called in to the station. The guy weighed his options and decided to take to his heels."

"He won't be easy to catch," said Augello. "As one of the Cuffaro gang, he'll be protected."

"You really think so?"

Fazio came in.

"How'd it go with Loredana?"

"I got her at the supermarket."

"Did she make a scene?"

"Nah, among other reasons because I didn't tell her I had a warrant for her arrest. All I said was that Prosecutor Tommaseo wanted to see her at once. She called the chief clerk, told her to close up when it was time, and then came quietly with me. I don't think any of the customers noticed anything. But I had the impression that she herself was expecting it."

"Maybe Valeria told not only Rosario but her too about being called in by the police."

"It's been a good day," said Fazio.

"Yes. And I thank you both. But now, if you don't mind, I'm gonna head home. It's late."

18

As he arrived in a flash outside his front door, he could hear the goddamned telephone ringing. He reached for the keys he usually kept in his left jacket pocket, but didn't find them.

The telephone stopped ringing.

Cursing and sweating, he searched every pocket. Nothing.

The telephone started ringing again.

He opened the car door and looked inside. No keys. They must have fallen out of his pocket at the office, when he took out the audio recorder.

He had an idea. He went down to the beach, circled round behind the house, climbed up onto the veranda, and pushed the French door. It was locked from the inside.

The phone, as if to spite him, started ringing again.

He raced back to the car, got inside, and headed back to Vigàta, driving as if he'd drunk a whole cask of wine. He very nearly had an accident and dodged four potentially violent encounters with enraged motorists before he pulled into the police parking lot. He got out, went in, and was blocked by Catarella.

"Ah, Chief! Iss a good ting yer 'ere! *Matre santa*, I been tryin' a ring yiz f'rever onna tiliphone!"

"That was you who was calling?"

"Yessir."

He heaved a sigh of relief. It hadn't been Marian.

"Why?"

"Cuz I wannit t'inform yiz o' the fack that ya forgat yer keys inni office."

"Wait a second, Cat. If you knew I forgot my keys, how could I have answered my phone?"

"Sorry, Chief, bu' how'z I asposta know 'at you wuz previnnit from ans'rin' yer phone?"

Montalbano gave up.

"Okay, okay, just gimme the keys," he said.

Once inside, he promised himself that he wouldn't go and see what Adelina had prepared for him before he had news from Marian.

He went out on the veranda and sat down. It was already five minutes to ten. He decided to wait until ten, and if Marian hadn't called by then, he would call her himself.

At that very moment the phone rang. It was Livia. He couldn't help but feel a little disappointed.

"How are you feeling?" he asked her straight off.

"I don't know."

"What do you mean?"

"Salvo, as I told you, I was in the grip of an oppressive, obscure anguish, an unbearable weight. Then, around six o'clock this evening, the anguish suddenly vanished."

"Finally!"

"Wait. Then, immediately afterwards, a sort of resignation took its place, as if there was nothing more to be done about anything, as if what I'd been fearing had actually and irreversibly occurred. The whole thing was accompanied by a feeling of very painful emptiness that can never be filled. The same as when you're in mourning. All I could do was cry. And I did nothing else. But crying gave me a kind of comfort."

"Naturally you didn't go to the doctor's, even though you promised me."

"I really don't think there's any need."

"Come on! With the condition you're in and—"

"Believe me, Salvo, I'll get over this, I can feel it. With effort and pain, yes, but I will get over it. Now I have to go. I don't feel like talking, it tires me out. All I want is to lie in bed. We'll talk again tomorrow."

In spite of everything, he felt reassured. There was a new note in Livia's voice that lent hope.

Now it was ten after ten. He was trembling with anticipation. Unable to wait any longer, he called Marian up on her cell phone.

He was agitated and twice dialed the wrong number. On the third try he finally got it right.

"My dear Inspector, I was about to call you myself."

"How are you feeling?"

He realized he'd used the same words he had with Livia.

"Pretty well, now. Really well. After the fright you gave me this morning . . ."

"I'm sorry, but—"

"I'm not reproaching you, Salvo. On the contrary . . ."

"Come on, tell me a little."

"Strazzeri is truly a lovely person. He made me feel reassured."

"Tell me everything in detail."

"After I called him up he was kind enough to come to my place. I told him the whole story, down to the last detail. He thought it over briefly and then said I should call Lariani and give him an ultimatum: Either he tells me something definitive by six p.m., or I drop everything."

"And what did Lariani say?"

"He joked around a little, reproached me for being impatient, but then said he'd call me back at six."

"And did he?"

"Yes. He gave me an appointment for tomorrow morning at eleven, at his place. He will show me the painting he says he's found, but which according to Strazzeri he must have retrieved from whoever was secretly holding it."

"Did you inform Strazzeri?"

"He was with me the whole time I was on the phone!"

"So how did you leave things?"

"Tomorrow morning at eleven I'm going alone to Lariani's. If he shows me the right painting, that is, the doctored one, Strazzeri showed me what to do without arousing any suspicion: All I have to do is press the button on a paging device I'll have in my pocket. And at that point the police will burst in. One of the officers' jobs is to get me out of there."

"But how will they explain your presence there when the case comes to trial?"

"In his report Strazzeri will write that I'm an undercover agent whose identity he's not at liberty to reveal."

"Well, that's excellent, don't you think?"

"Yes, I think so too."

A second later, Montalbano was overcome by doubt.

"Are you sure you'll be able to deal with Lariani all by yourself?"

"Of course I'll be able, don't worry."

"Don't you think it's a little risky?"

"Strazzeri and his men will be very close by. At the first sign of danger, all I have to do is press the button."

"Listen, as soon as they take you away, please send me a message on my cell phone."

"Okay, Salvo, but please don't worry. I'll be brave and determined, if only so I can get out of there. And thank you, dear Inspector, for saving me. But how did you come to realize that Lariani wasn't what he appeared to be?"

He told her about seeing the graffiti on the metal shutter.

"And that Pedicini!" said Marian. "He seemed so respectable! And he was so clever in winning my trust! He must have spent a fortune!"

"Apparently the painting you were supposed to bring him from Milan is worth a great deal more."

Marian, however, was already thinking of other things.

"There's a flight for Palermo tomorrow afternoon at five. Shall we have dinner together tomorrow night? Are you free?"

"As a matter of fact, I think I am."

"I'm counting the hours, my dear Inspector. I'm so happy. And tomorrow evening I'll be even happier. Does nine o'clock at your place sound okay?"

"It sounds perfect."

"Promise to wait for me if I'm a little late?"

"I promise."

When the phone call was over, he headed for the kitchen, singing the triumphal march from *Aida*. He decided to play a game. He would close his eyes and try to guess from the aroma what Adelina had made for him. The refrigerator smelled empty. When he opened the oven, his nostrils immediately filled with a breathtaking, twofold aroma. It didn't take him long to tell the one from the other: *tagliatelle al ragù* and eggplant Parmesan. Could one really expect any more out of life?

He ate on the veranda, taking his time because he wanted to watch the midnight news report. When he'd finished eating, he cleared the table, turned on the television, and sat down in the armchair with his cigarettes within reach. He watched a string of ads, after which the Free Channel's news report logo came on the screen, and then Zito appeared.

"We begin our report tonight with an item that came in right at the end of our ten o'clock report and which we were unable to present for lack of time. In the Savastano murder case, the investigating magistrate Antonio Grasso has failed to confirm the arrest of Salvatore di Marta, until now the prime suspect. We have also learned that Public Prosecutor Tommaseo will not appeal the decision, and as a result, di Marta was immediately released. The prosecutor, however, was keen to point out that di Marta remains nevertheless under investigation. But it's clear at this point that if subsequent investigation does not yield any solid evidence of di Marta's guilt, all charges will be dropped and the case will once again be in no-man's-land.

"We also have another important development to report, for which, however, we have not yet received any official confirmation. The word is that the hunt for the three immigrants that has gone on for several days has come to an at least partial conclusion. Apparently two of the three men have been arrested. They have thus far refused to answer any of the investigators' questions, shutting themselves up behind a wall of silence. As to the fate of the third man, the one armed with a machine gun and believed to be wounded, we know nothing at this time. As soon as we have more verifiable information on this case, which thus far has seemed fairly murky to us, we will bring it at once to the attention of our viewing audience.

"A fatal accident occurred this afternoon around four o'clock on the provincial road to . . ."

He turned it off. So nobody knew yet that the Savastano murder investigation was over. Tommaseo had been shrewd to say that di Marta was still a suspect. It was clearly a move intended to let the fugitive Rosario relax a little, in the hope that he would make a false move.

Mimì's words came back to him, when he said that Rosario would be hard to catch because he had the Cuffaros' protection. Except that the Cuffaros didn't know the truth yet. Still . . . there was in fact a way to let them discover it.

Montalbano smiled at the thought. He looked at his watch. It was twenty past midnight. Too early. He should call at one at the very earliest. He shuffled about the house a little, then decided to take a shower and get ready for bed.

When he picked up the phone it was ten past one. He dialed the number.

"Hello? Who is this?" a sleepy male voice asked in irritation.

"Am I speaking with Guttadauro the lawyer?"

"Yes, but who is this?"

"Montalbano."

Guttadauro's tone of voice immediately changed.

"Good Inspector! To what do I owe—"

"Forgive me for calling at this hour—I'm sure I woke you up—but since I'm about to leave, I decided that calling you at the crack of dawn would be worse."

"Not at all, there's no excuse necessary. You were right to call!"

The lawyer was clearly dying of curiosity to know why the inspector had called, but he didn't want to take the initiative.

Montalbano decided to tweak him a little.

"How are you?"

"Fine, fine. And you?"

"Not too bad, but for the past few days I've had a rather bothersome itch."

Guttadauro politely refrained from asking where he had the itch.

"You said you were about to leave," he said instead. "Going anywhere interesting?"

"I'm taking a few days off, now that the Savastano case has been closed."

"Closed? What do you mean?" asked a confused Guttadauro. "If di Marta remains under investigation despite being released, that means the case hasn't—"

"I'm surprised at you, counsel! With all your experience . . . Rest assured, if I say the case has been closed, it's been closed."

"Then who was the killer?"

"Now, now, counsel, that has to remain a secret!"

"But couldn't you—"

"Are you joking, sir?"

"All right, I won't insist. But then . . ."

"Then what?"

Guttadauro was at the breaking point.

"No, I meant . . ."

"Go ahead, I'm listening."

Montalbano was having a ball. Guttadauro finally broke.

"Then why did you call me?"

"Ah, yes. I almost forgot."

The inspector started laughing.

"Why are you laughing?" asked Guttadauro, getting upset.

"Do remember the little story you told me the other day? The one about the lion hunter? Well, just this evening I heard it again, but with some notable variants."

"What kind of variants?"

"Well, for one thing, these lion hunters were in an area in which lion hunting was prohibited."

"And what does that imply?"

"It implies that a very young hunter, a novice, from Montereale, who'd just joined the club—and not just any native, as in your version—killed a lion on his own, without telling the other hunters, and then arranged things so that the killing would be blamed on his comrades and not on him. Is that clear?"

Guttadauro paused before answering. He was trying to grasp the meaning of the inspector's words. At last he did. He said only:

"Ah."

"Is that clear?" Montalbano repeated.

"Perfectly," Guttadauro said curtly.

"Then all that's left for me to do is to wish you a good, refreshing sleep."

It was done. Guttadauro was surely already on the telephone, informing the Cuffaros that Rosario had strayed. The kid's fate was sealed.

If he didn't turn himself in to the police, he would be murdered by his former playmates.

The inspector went to bed and fell asleep as soon as his head touched the pillow.

The ringing of the telephone brought him up from the depths of a veritable abyss. He turned on the light: It was six a.m.

"Montalbano? This is Sposìto."

He balked. What could Sposìto want from him at that hour?

"What is it?"

"Can you be ready in half an hour?"

"Yes, but—"

"I'll be there at six-thirty to pick you up."

And he hung up. Montalbano lay there bewildered, receiver in hand. What had happened? No point in wondering, for now. The only thing to do was to get ready, and fast. He opened the window and looked out at the sky.

The weather promised to be variable and capricious that morning. And therefore, by contagion, the inspector's behavior would likewise be unstable at the very least.

He went and got into the shower. At six-thirty he was ready. A minute later there was a knock at the door. He opened it. There was a uniformed cop, who greeted him. Montalbano went out and locked the door behind him. Sposìto had him sit in the back beside him. The policeman sat down at the wheel and drove off.

"What's going on?" asked Montalbano.

"I'd rather not say anything until we get there," said Sposìto.

Was it something to do with the Tunisians they said were arrested the day before? And if so, why was Sposìto dragging him into the thick of it, after he'd done everything in his power to keep him out of it?

They turned off the main road and drove along dirt paths fit for tanks and little country roads less wide than the car itself. The sky had gone from a pale pink to gray, and then from gray had turned a faded blue before settling momentarily on a foggy whitishness that blurred outlines and muddled one's vision. Montalbano now knew where they were going; he'd figured it out a ways back.

"Are we going to the Casuzza district?" he asked.

"Do you know the place?" Sposìto inquired.

"Yes."

He'd been there twice, the first time in a dream, to go and see a coffin, and the second in reality, to go and see a charred car with a murdered man inside. What would Sposìto have him see this time?

The moment they arrived, Montalbano's blood ran cold.

In the exact same spot where there had been a coffin in the dream, there now was a real one, an exact replica of the one he'd dreamt. A coffin for third-class cadavers, the poorest of the poor, of rough-hewn wood without so much as a coat of varnish.

A corner of white linen stuck out from under the lid, which had been laid down crooked.

A short distance away was another police car with three cops inside, and a black hearse. The two attendants paced about beside the car, smoking.

There was total silence. Montalbano clenched his teeth. He was living a sort of nightmare. He looked questioningly at Sposìto, at which point the latter put his arm around the inspector affectionately and pulled him aside.

"Inside that box is one of the three Tunisians. I've been ordered to send the body to Tunisia. But before I do, I wanted you to see it. The man inside was not an arms smuggler, but a patriot. He died of complications from the wound he suffered during the entirely involuntary exchange of fire with my men. I'd been following him for a while. I knew everything about him, even his private life, but he remained elusive. When you see him you'll understand why I wanted to keep you out of this. It was he who recognized you that day when he was hiding out in the hayloft. He was watching you through a pair of binoculars."

The beam of light that had struck him square in the eyes.

In confused fashion, Montalbano began to understand but refused to accept it. He couldn't move. Sposìto nudged him gently towards the coffin.

"Be brave," he said.

The inspector bent down, gripped the linen between his thumb and index finger, and pulled it out a little further. Now he could see the letters *F* and *M* intertwined.

His legs began to give out; he fell to his knees.

F.M.: François Moussa. He'd had those initials embroidered himself on six shirts he'd given to François as a present for his twenty-first birthday. It was the last time he'd embraced him.

"Would you like to see him?" Sposìto asked softly, whispering in his ear.

"No."

He would rather his last contact with François remain the beam of light that had brought them together again for a fraction of a second.

And if he wanted every now and then to remember him, he would content himself with the time when, as a little boy of ten, François had run away from the house in Marinella, and Livia, who by that point considered him her own son, sounded the alarm and he ran after the boy along the beach, catching up with him and finally stopping him. They had a talk. François said he wanted his mother Karima, who was dead, and so Montalbano told him how he, too, had lost his mother when he was even younger than François. In fact he told him things he'd never revealed to anyone, not even Livia. And from that moment on, they'd understood each other.

Then, as the years went by, distance and detachment had settled in . . .

He had nothing more to do or say in front of the coffin. He stood up and leaned on Sposito's arm.

"Could you have someone give me a ride back?" he asked.

"Of course."

"Listen, has Pasquano already been here?"

"Yes."

"Was he able to determine the time of death?"

"Approximately around six p.m. yesterday."

"Thanks for everything," said Montalbano, getting into a car.

Six p.m. *Then, around six o'clock this evening, the anguish suddenly vanished, and a sort of resignation took its place, as if there was nothing more to be done about anything . . .*

Without knowing it, Livia had suffered François's agony and death in her own body and soul, as if he'd been a son, of her own flesh and blood. A son which he, Montalbano, out of selfishness and a fear of responsibility, hadn't wanted them to adopt. Livia had taken it very hard. But he'd remained firm in his refusal.

Now he knew what he had to do. Through his death, François bound him to Livia and Livia to him even more than if they were married.

When he got home he phoned the commissioner's office and asked for a ten-day leave. He had a great backlog of vacation days, and they were happy to grant him the time. He reserved a seat on the first flight for Genoa, which was at two o'clock in the afternoon. Lastly he called Fazio, told him Livia wasn't doing well, and that he was going to spend a few days with her.

He sat down on the veranda and smoked a few cigarettes, thinking of François. Then he stood up, wiped his eyes with his shirtsleeve, and went and started leisurely packing.

That same evening at nine o'clock, Marian knocked a long time at his front door, which she didn't know would never be open for her again.

Author's Note

This novel is completely made up. It follows that all the characters, names, and situations do not and cannot refer to any real people or situations in which they may have found themselves at one time or another during their lives. Despite this disclaimer, which I am keen to repeat conscientiously at the end of every one of my novels, now and then someone comes out thinking they recognize himself or herself in one of my characters, sometimes going so far as to threaten legal action. Perhaps such people are unsatisfied with their own reality.

Notes

11   a solitary little house, perhaps the one that lent the place its name: In Italian (with a Sicilian diminutive) *casuzza* means "little house."

18–19   He was convinced that Catarella had only made his way, barely, through the compulsory years of schooling: School in Italy is compulsory up to age sixteen.

28   Back in 1996 they'd had to take a little Tunisian orphan of ten into their home: For the full story of young François, see the third book in the Montalbano series, *The Snack Thief* (Penguin, 2003), also available in *Death in Sicily* (Penguin, 2013), an omnibus edition comprising the first three novels of the series.

38   Apparently the passengers had wanted to visit the Greek temples: The fictional town of Montelusa is modeled on the real-world city of Agrigento (Girgenti in Sicilian), which boasts of the largest archaeological site in the world, the Valle de' Templi (Valley of the Temples), a complex of seven Greek temples in the Doric style, most from the fifth century B.C., in varying degrees of conservation. The best preserved is the Temple of Concordia, one of the most intact Greek temples in the world today.

72 Don't the police ever talk to the carabinieri? Or the carabinieri to the police?: The carabinieri are a national police force and officially a branch of the army (like the gendarmes in France and the Guardia Civil in Spain). They have sweeping jurisdictional powers but are often in competition with the Commissariati di Pubblica Sicurezza, the branch of law enforcement that Montalbano is part of. As a result, the two bureaucracies sometimes do not communicate with each other, especially when one fears that the other may gain the upper hand on a given case.

134 they rent a little room in the Rabato: The Rabato was the Arab quarter of Agrigento (the model for Camilleri's fictional Montelusa) during the Middle Ages and in recent times has been favored by the new waves of Arab immigrants to Sicily.

255 a municipal cop: In Italy, the municipal police (Vigili Urbani) are a separate jurisdiction from the *commissariati* (such as Montalbano's outfit), which handle criminal investigations.

265 the Catturandi: The Catturandi are an elite police unit charged with finding and capturing members of the Mafia, particularly longtime fugitives from the law.

Notes by Stephen Sartarelli

Andrea Camilleri, a bestseller in Italy and Germany, is the author of the popular Inspector Montalbano mystery series as well as historical novels that take place in nineteenth-century Sicily. His books have been made into Italian TV shows and translated into thirty-two languages. His thirteenth Montalbano novel, *The Potter's Field*, won the Crime Writers' Association International Dagger Award and was long-listed for the IMPAC Dublin Literary Award.

Stephen Sartarelli is an award-winning translator and the author of three books of poetry.

Center Point Large Print
600 Brooks Road / PO Box 1
Thorndike, ME 04986-0001 USA

(207) 568-3717

US & Canada:
1 800 929-9108
www.centerpointlargeprint.com